MACMILLAN READERS
INTERMEDIATE LEVEL

SUE GRAFTON

"A" is for Alibi

Retold by John Escott

INTERMEDIATE LEVEL

Founding Editor: John Milne

The Macmillan Readers provide a choice of enjoyable reading materials for learners of English. The series is published at six levels – Starter, Beginner, Elementary, Pre-intermediate, Intermediate and Upper.

Level control
Information, structure and vocabulary are controlled to suit the students' ability at each level.

The number of words at each level:

Starter	about 300 basic words
Beginner	about 600 basic words
Elementary	about 1100 basic words
Pre-intermediate	about 1400 basic words
Intermediate	about 1600 basic words
Upper	about 2200 basic words

Vocabulary
Some difficult words and phrases in this book are important for understanding the story. Some of these words are explained in the story and some are shown in the pictures. From Pre-intermediate level upwards, words are marked with a number like this: ...[3]. These words are explained in the Glossary at the end of the book.

Contents

Notes About the Author and This Story

Sue Grafton was born on April 24th, 1940, in Louisville, Kentucky in the U.S.A. Her father, C.W. Grafton, was a writer of mystery stories. Before she became a novelist, Sue Grafton wrote scripts for TV plays.

"A" is for Alibi was her first crime detection novel. The main character of the story is Kinsey Millhone, a thirty-two-year-old female private detective[1]. After "A" is for Alibi, Sue Grafton wrote "B" is for Burglar and "C" is for Corpse which are also about Kinsey's cases. The author is going to write twenty-six stories about Kinsey Millhone, one for each letter of the alphabet.

Sue Grafton now lives with her husband in Santa Barbara, California.

In this story, Kinsey Millhone lives and works in a town called Santa Teresa in southern California. Santa Teresa is not a real town, but most of the other places that Kinsey visits are real. Some of them are in the state of Nevada, to the east of California. California is a large state on the west coast of the U.S.A.

The People in This Story

Kinsey Millhone

Nikki Fife

Gwen Fife

Greg, Diane and Colin Fife

Charlie Scorsoni

Charlotte Mercer

Raymond and Grace Glass

Lyle Abernathy

Sharon Napier

Garry Steinberg

Lieutenant Dolan

Ruth, a secretary at Scorsoni and Powers
Arlette, the manager of the Hacienda Motor Lodge

5

1
Nikki Fife

My name is Kinsey Millhone and I'm a private detective. I'm thirty-two years old, and I live and work in Santa Teresa, in southern California. I live alone in a small apartment. I've been married twice, but my second husband and I were divorced some years ago.

The day before yesterday, I killed someone. I had to do it, but knowing that doesn't make me happy. I'm a nice person. People like me. I have a lot of friends. Killing someone has made me feel bad.

I've already given a signed statement[2] about the death to the police. I've also written a report for the client[3] that I was working for. But now I want to tell the whole story.

Nikki Fife first came to my office one day at the beginning of May. That was less than three weeks ago. My office is quite small—just two rooms with a view of Santa Teresa's main street. I use an answering service[4]—somebody takes my phone calls when I'm out of my office. I don't have a secretary.

I'd been out for most of the morning and Nikki Fife was standing by my office door when I got back. I'd never talked to Nikki before, but I'd been at her trial eight years earlier. Nikki Fife had been sent to jail for murdering her husband, Laurence, a successful Santa Teresa divorce attorney[5].

Nikki was twenty-seven or twenty-eight years old when she was jailed. At that time, she'd had white-blond hair, dark eyes and perfect skin. Now, her face was a little fatter, and her hair was its real color—very light brown.

I didn't say anything at first, I just unlocked my office

door and let her in.

"You know who I am," she said.

"Yes. I worked for your husband a few times," I replied. "Would you like some coffee?"

She nodded. "Yes, please."

I made some coffee for both of us.

"When did you get out of jail?" I asked her.

"A week ago," she said. "I didn't kill Laurence. I want you to find out who did."

I wasn't surprised. I'd never believed that Nikki Fife was guilty[6].

"I was married to Laurence for more than four years," she went on. She drank some coffee, then put the cup on the edge of my desk. "We'd only been married for six months when he had an affair[7] with another woman. And he had several affairs after that. I didn't like it. But I don't know why I was so surprised about it—he'd had an affair with me while he was married to his first wife."

"People said that you killed him *because* of his affairs with other women," I told her.

"You kill people that you hate," Nikki replied, "or you kill because you're angry. You don't kill somebody that you don't care about. I didn't care about Laurence. I stopped loving him when I found out about that first affair. By that time, I was going to have a baby, and I didn't want to leave him. But I didn't worry about his affairs after that."

"Who do *you* think killed Laurence?" I asked.

"I think a lot of people *wanted* to kill him. I could make some guesses about who did it. But I can't prove anything. That's why I'm here."

"Why did you come to me?"

7

"*I want you to find out who killed Laurence.*"

"I talked to Lieutenant Dolan, at the Santa Teresa Police Department. It was his idea."

"Dolan investigated your husband's murder, didn't he?" I asked.

Nikki nodded. "Yes. He said that you'd remember the case. I don't like having to explain everything from the beginning."

"Does Dolan think that you're innocent?"

"Probably not. But I've done my time[8] in jail, so he can't stop me from trying to find out the truth."

I looked at her carefully.

"Let me think about this for a while," I said.

Nikki Fife took some old newspaper reports out of her bag. "I'll leave these with you," she said. "And here's my phone number."

She gave me a piece of paper with a number written on it.

"I'll call you later today," I told her.

———

I didn't really need to look at the newspaper reports—I remembered the facts of the case well. Laurence Fife was thirty-nine years old when he died. On the evening of his murder, he'd gone to a bar with Charlie Scorsoni, his partner in the law firm of Fife and Scorsoni. He arrived home at about midnight—the Fifes lived in the Montebello area of Santa Teresa. Laurence had to take medicine for several allergies[9]. Before he went to bed that night, he took a medicine capsule[10]. By the morning, he was dead.

The police investigation showed that the allergy medicine had been removed from the capsule, and replaced with powdered oleander[11]. The leaves of the oleander bush are very poisonous. There was an oleander bush in the Fifes'

9

garden, although it's true that they grow everywhere in California. If Nikki did kill her husband, she didn't have to go far for the poison. Her fingerprints[12] were found on the medicine bottle which had contained the capsules, together with Laurence's own fingerprints. And Nikki's diary showed that she knew about Laurence's affairs, that she was angry about them, and that she was thinking about divorcing him.

Laurence had been married and divorced once before. And because he was a divorce attorney, he'd known how to get the best result for himself at his divorce hearing[13]. His first wife had received very little money, and their two children had gone to live with Laurence.

Nikki, who had a four-year-old son at the time of Laurence's murder, knew about his first wife's problems. Lieutenant Dolan had said that this was the reason why Nikki decided to kill her husband instead of divorcing him. She wanted to keep Laurence's money, and she didn't want him to take her young son away from her.

I'd thought that Dolan was wrong. I didn't believe that Nikki had wanted money. She came from a very rich family and she had a lot of money of her own. And I didn't believe that Laurence could have taken her son away from her. There had to be a special reason why Fife's first wife hadn't kept her children.

I thought about all this, and I decided that I wanted to help Nikki Fife.

––––

Santa Teresa is a town of eighty thousand people. A lot of them are very rich. The town lies between the Sierra Madre mountains and the Pacific Ocean. It's a beautiful place, with tall palm trees and brightly colored flowers along the sides of the streets. The police department is near the center of the town. And that's where I went next. I know the police department well, because I used to work there. I was once a police officer myself.

Lieutenant Dolan knew why I had come, and he took me to his office.

"How can I help you, Kinsey?" he asked. He didn't sound like a man who wanted to help me.

"I'd like to look at the report on the Laurence Fife murder investigation," I said.

He smiled but his eyes were cold. "She killed him, Kinsey," he said.

"You told Nikki to come and see me," I replied. "So maybe you aren't sure that Nikki was guilty—you have doubts, is that right?"

"My doubts have nothing to do with Laurence Fife's death," he said. He stared at me for a moment, then picked up his phone. "This is Dolan," he said into it. "Bring me the report on Laurence Fife."

He put the phone down and looked at me. "Listen, Kinsey," he said. "I'll let you see the report. But I don't want to hear any complaints about the way that you investigate this! Do you understand me? No complaints—not from family members, not from *my* men, not from any other police department. OK?"

The papers arrived and he gave them to me. "You can read them in Lieutenant Becker's office," he told me.

It took me two hours to read through all the papers, but almost the first things that I found were some notes from the West Los Angeles Police Department about another murder. An accountant[14] named Libby Glass, aged twenty-four, had died four days after Laurence Fife. The cause of her death? Oleander poisoning!

Libby Glass had worked for Haycraft and McNiece, a business management company that looked after the accounts of Laurence Fife's law firm. Laurence and Libby must have known each other. And when the police had searched Fife's office desk, a week after he was killed, they'd found a key to Libby's apartment in it. Now what did all that tell me?

I read quickly through the detectives' reports, trying to understand the story. Libby Glass's boyfriend, a young man named Lyle Abernathy, had thought that Libby was having an affair with someone else. "She was meeting a lawyer from Santa Teresa," he'd told the police. But nobody learned much more than that about her life.

I wrote down the address and phone number of Libby's parents and also the number of the company where her boyfriend had worked. Then I left Becker's office.

Lieutenant Dolan was walking along the corridor towards me.

"Did you think that Nikki Fife killed Libby Glass, too?" I asked him.

"Yes, but I couldn't prove it," he said. "We worked on the investigation for months. So did the West Los Angeles Police Department, but they couldn't prove anything either. If Fife had a key to Libby Glass's apartment, he must have been having an affair with her. We thought that Nikki had found out about it, and killed Libby as well as Laurence. But we couldn't prove that Nikki Fife *knew* about Libby Glass."

"And now you think that I'm going to help you. You want *me* to prove that Nikki killed her!" I said.

12

"You might prove it," Dolan replied. "And if you do prove it, you'll tell me. You're an honest investigator. You're young, but you're honest."

"Lieutenant, if Nikki is guilty, why has she asked me to start a new investigation into her husband's death?" I said. "I don't believe that she killed Laurence. So it's going to be difficult to make me believe that she killed someone else too!"

———

I called Nikki from my apartment and I asked her to meet me for a drink. We met at a bar called Rosie's, and I told her what I had read about the murder of Libby Glass.

"Did you know about her?" I asked.

Nikki shook her head. "No. But my lawyer did tell me about her, during the trial."

"You never heard Laurence speak about her? You never saw her name written down anywhere?" I asked.

"Well, I never found any letters from her in Laurence's pockets, if that's what you mean," she said. "But he was having an affair with *someone* just before he died."

"Did his lovers visit him at his office?"

"I don't know. Ask Charlie Scorsoni," Nikki said. "Charlie's still here in Santa Teresa. He has a new law partner—a man named John Powers."

"OK. Tell me something, Nikki. Why did you stay married to Laurence?"

"I was going to divorce him, but there was—"

"Your son?" I said.

"Yes. His name's Colin. He's twelve now and he's been staying at a school near Monterey."

"You also had Laurence's other kids living with you at the time of Laurence's death, didn't you?" I asked.

13

"Yes," she replied. "A boy and a girl, Greg and Diane. They were both in high school then."

"Where are they now?"

"I don't know. But Laurence's first wife, Gwen, still lives here in town. You could ask her."

"Did the older kids blame[15] you for their father's death?"

"Everyone blamed me. Greg and Diane haven't called me or written to me since I got out of jail. Lieutenant Dolan thinks that I killed Libby Glass too. Am I right?"

"I don't care what Dolan thinks," I said. "I'm going to work on this case. Where do I start?"

"Speak to Charlie. And maybe you should speak to the woman who was Laurence's secretary. Her name was Sharon Napier. She'd been working for him for some years when I first met him. But there was something—something wrong about her."

"Was she one of his lovers?" I asked.

"No, I don't think that she *was* one of his lovers," Nikki replied, after a moment. "But she had some kind of power over[16] Laurence. She was often rude to him, and she wouldn't work late, or work on weekends when he had an important trial. He never complained about her, and that was strange! Laurence usually complained if people didn't do what he wanted. Sharon was a very beautiful young woman, and she always wore expensive clothes. But she didn't earn enough money at the law firm to buy clothes like that."

"Do you know where she lives?" I asked.

Nikki shook her head.

"Well, I'll try to find out about her," I said.

Nikki gave me a check for five thousand dollars, as my first payment for the case.

14

2

Gwen Fife

The offices of Charlie Scorsoni's law firm, Scorsoni and Powers, were only a short distance from my own office, so I walked there the next afternoon. I had to wait to see Charlie Scorsoni. While I waited, I talked to the firm's secretary. Her name was Ruth.

"How long have you worked here?" I asked her.

"Seven years," she said. "I came here when Charlie Scorsoni and John Powers first became law partners."

She then told me how wonderful both men were. Forty-five minutes later, I met Charlie Scorsoni. He was a big man with sand-colored hair and blue eyes. He looked at me carefully, from head to foot, then he smiled slowly.

"Ruth tells me that you have some questions about Laurence Fife," he said.

"Yes. I've started a new investigation into his death. It seemed sensible to talk to you first," I said.

He pointed to a chair. "Please sit down," he said. "I heard that Nikki was out of jail. If she's told you that she didn't kill Laurence, she's crazy."

"I didn't say that I was working for Nikki," I said.

"Who else could you be working for?"

"You aren't very happy about my investigation?"

"Listen, Laurence was my best friend," the attorney said angrily. "Nikki killed him!"

"How did you first meet Laurence?" I asked.

"We were students together. We both studied at the University of Denver for a while. But his family had money, and mine had none. So Laurence went to study law at

15

Harvard. I went to Arizona State University. I didn't see him for a few years. But then I heard that he'd started a law firm here in Santa Teresa. I came here and I talked to him about working for his firm. He said OK. He made me a partner in the firm two years later."

"Was he married to his first wife then?"

"Yes, her name's Gwen. She still lives here in town. You could talk to her, but she's got nothing good to say about Laurence. She's got a business on State Street. It's a dog grooming business—she makes dogs look pretty! The place is called K9 Korners[17]!"

Charlie was watching me carefully.

"What do you know about Sharon Napier?" I asked him. "How long did she work for Laurence?"

"She was working for him when I first came to the firm," he replied. "She stayed until Nikki's trial was finished, then she left. She owes me some money, so if you find her, please tell me where she is."

"Do you know about Libby Glass?" I asked. "She was the accountant who looked after your firm's accounts. She worked for Haycraft and McNiece in Los Angeles."

Charlie thought for a moment, then shook his head.

"No, I don't know anything about her. Why do you ask about her?"

"She was also killed with oleander, at about the same time that Laurence died," I replied. "And Laurence had a key to her apartment." Charlie didn't look surprised. "You never met her?" I went on.

"I *must* have met her, if she worked on our accounts," he replied. "But I don't *remember* her. I probably did meet her once or twice, but Laurence usually saw the business managers."

"Maybe he was having an affair with her?" I said.

Charlie smiled, then he looked at his watch. "I'm sorry to stop you, but it's four-fifteen and I have some work to finish before I leave."

I stood up. "Thanks for talking to me," I said. I smiled at him and shook his hand. He seemed to be a nice man. I liked him.

He walked to the door and held it open for me.

"Good luck," he said. "But I don't expect that you'll discover anything new."

———

The next morning, I left my apartment at 9 a.m., and I drove north in my old cream-colored Volkswagen. By the time I found K9 Korners, it was 9:15. As I walked through the door, I heard the noise of dogs barking. There were several grooming rooms near the door and I could see a woman washing a dog in one of them. She looked up and saw me.

"Can I help you?" she asked. She was a tall woman, in her mid-forties, with large brown eyes and long gray hair.

"Are you Gwen Fife?" I asked her.

The woman had a friendly smile. "Yes, that's right," she replied.

"I'm Kinsey Millhone. I'm a private investigator."

Gwen laughed. "Oh! Why are you here?"

"I understand that you were married to Laurence Fife," I said.

"Yes," she replied. "Is this about Laurence? He's been dead for years."

"I know that. I'm starting a new investigation into his death."

"Oh, that's interesting," she said. "Who are you working for?"

"Nikki," I replied. "Will you answer some questions for me?"

"Can we talk while I work on the dog?" she asked. "We're very busy today."

"That's OK, Gwen," I said. "How long were you married to Laurence Fife?"

"Thirteen years. We met at college. I was a good wife to him. I spent all that time trying to make him happy. When our marriage ended, I was very angry."

"What went wrong?"

Gwen's face went red. She didn't answer for a moment. Then she smiled again. "I'll tell you about that later, if you're really interested."

"OK, that's fine."

"Oh, I don't blame Laurence for everything that went wrong," she said. "But I don't blame myself for everything either. My life was very difficult after the divorce. I didn't have much money. And my kids went to live with Laurence."

"But the kids must have come back to you after Laurence died and Nikki was sent to jail," I said.

"Yes, but they were nearly old enough to go to college by then. And they were very unhappy kids, after living with Laurence for five years. He was a difficult father to live with and a difficult man to love."

"Are they here in town now?" I asked her.

"No. Greg's living at Salton Sea. He's got a boat on the lake."

"What kind of work does he do?"

"Well, he doesn't do anything. He doesn't *have* to do

18

"…My life was very difficult after the divorce…"

anything," she said. "Laurence was rich and he left all his money to[18] his three kids—Greg, Diane, and his and Nikki's son, Colin."

"Where's Diane?" I asked.

"She's gone back to college. She's at a college in Claremont," Gwen told me. "She wants to teach deaf[19] children. When she first told me about it, I thought that it was because of Colin, but—"

"Colin?" I said. I was surprised.

"Didn't Nikki tell you that Colin was deaf?" she asked. "He was born deaf. Diane was very upset about that. She was thirteen when Colin was born. Diane's a good kid. Greg's a good kid too. He used to take drugs, but I think that he's OK now. I'm sure that he'll find some work soon."

"Would it be OK if I talked to them?" I asked.

Gwen looked worried. "You want to talk to them about their father? Well—*maybe* it would be all right. I'm not sure. Can I think about this?"

"OK. We can talk about it another time," I said. "Maybe I won't *need* to speak to them."

"I really don't understand why you're investigating all this again," she said. "Nikki killed Laurence, didn't she? There were times when I wanted to kill him myself. Laurence was a cruel man. People often say to me, 'Thank God that he's dead.' That's the truth, Kinsey!"

"Who?" I asked her quickly. "Who says that?"

She laughed. "If you have an hour, I'll give you a list."

I laughed too. "Could we could talk again soon?"

"I finish working here at six," she said. "Maybe we can have a drink then."

"OK. I'll see you here at six," I said.

3

Charlie Scorsoni

I went to a phone booth[20] and I called Nikki.
"Nikki? This is Kinsey. Can I see the house in Montebello where you and Laurence used to live?"

"Of course," she said. "It was always my house and I still own it. I'm going to drive to Monterey today. I'm going to bring Colin back to Santa Teresa. But I'll meet you at the house before I leave town. I'll meet you there in twenty minutes." She told me the address.

Montebello is the part of town where the richest people live. You can't see the houses from the roads there, because they all have big yards with grass, trees and high walls. The Fifes' house was a very large one, on a corner. I parked my car outside it and, soon after, Nikki stopped behind me in hers. We both got out of our cars.

"Who had keys to this house eight years ago?" I asked, while Nikki was unlocking the front door.

"Laurence and me, Greg and Diane," she replied. "And we had a housekeeper[21]—Mrs Voss. She must have had a key."

We went inside the house. The rooms were large, with high ceilings. Everything was clean and tidy and silent. Upstairs, there were five bedrooms, all with bathrooms.

"Are you going to live in this house with Colin?" I asked, as we came down the stairs.

"I haven't stayed here since I got out of jail, but I might do that soon," Nikki said. "Someone comes in to clean the house every two weeks. I've been staying at my house at the beach since I got out of jail."

"Oh, you have another house in Santa Teresa?"

"Yes. Laurence's mother left the beach house to me when she died," she said. "She died about three years before Laurence was killed."

"Why did she leave the house to you and not to him?"

She smiled. "Laurence and his mother weren't very friendly with each other. And she liked me. Would you like some tea?"

I followed her into the kitchen.

"Who have you talked to about this case?" Nikki asked.

I told her about my conversation with Charlie Scorsoni while she made the tea. "Did you ever think that *he* might have killed Laurence?" I asked her.

She smiled. "I've thought about everyone. But Charlie? No, I don't think so. Maybe he did have a reason. But if he did, I don't know what it was."

Then I told her about my talk with Gwen. "Did Gwen divorce Laurence because he had an affair with you?" I asked.

"Oh, no," she said. "Laurence discovered that Gwen was having an affair herself. He had his affair with me to prove that he didn't care about *her* affair. But he punished her by taking the kids and the money from her."

I asked Nikki about the night that Laurence died.

"He was taking allergy medicine. What was he allergic to?" I asked her.

"Lots of things. Air pollution[22], animal hair," she replied. "Dog hair was the worst, but he was allergic to cat hair too. For a long time, he wouldn't have an animal in the house. But when Colin was two, we bought him a dog."

"Colin's deaf, isn't he?"

"Yes. He was born deaf," she replied sadly.

"And the dog was for him? Was it a guard dog[23]?"

"Yes. You can't watch a kid all the time, and Bruno looked after Colin. Laurence knew that Bruno was good for the boy. Laurence was a difficult man, but he did love Colin."

"Do you still have the dog?" I asked.

"No. Bruno was killed, years ago," Nikki said sadly. "He was hit by a car, just out there on the road, in front of this house." There was a tired look in her eyes now. "I hope that you do find out who killed Laurence, Kinsey. I'll never be happy until I know."

———

I went back to my office and I worked all afternoon, writing notes about the investigation. Then at 4:45, I went for a run on the road next to the beach. I ran for two miles, then I walked for a while. Suddenly, a big pale-blue Mercedes stopped beside me, and I saw Charlie Scorsoni smiling at me from the driver's seat.

"I felt sorry because I couldn't give you more help yesterday," he said. "Get in. I'll take you back to your apartment."

———

At my apartment, I had a shower and I got dressed. I realized that I was pleased to see Charlie Scorsoni. He was a good-looking man, his hair was nice, and I liked his blue eyes. And I don't often think that kind of thing about forty-eight-year-old men!

"Can I take you out for a drink?" he said, when I came into the living room.

"I have to be somewhere else at six o'clock," I answered. "Do you want to drink a beer here?"

"OK. I'd like that, Kinsey," he said.

I got him a beer from the fridge, then I sat down in a chair opposite him. "Why did you decide to visit me?"

"I have to leave town for a couple of days," he replied. "I have to go to Denver. But I wanted to see you. If Nikki didn't kill Laurence, I'd like to know who did."

"But you don't believe that Nikki's innocent."

"I believe that *you* believe it," he said. Charlie smiled at me. "I wasn't honest with you yesterday," he went on. "I *did* know who that girl in L.A. was—Libby Glass. And I also suspected[24] that Laurence was having an affair with her. But he was my friend and he was good to me. I didn't want *you* to know about my suspicions. Then today, I decided that it might be important for you to know."

"What was Libby like?" I asked.

"I met her only a few times. She seemed nice. She was young—no more than twenty-five or twenty-six."

"Did Laurence tell you that he was having an affair with her?"

"Oh, no. But he never spoke to me about his women."

"You went out for a drink with him on the night that he died, didn't you?" I asked.

"Yes, that's right. And in fact, we had dinner together."

"Did he have the allergy medicine with him then?"

Scorsoni shook his head. "Nikki said that he took the allergy capsule after he got home," he replied. "She said that at the trial."

"Had Libby Glass visited him that day?" I asked.

"I don't know, Kinsey," he replied after a moment. "If she had, he never said anything to me about it. Why do you want to know?"

"Well, I had an idea," I said. "I was thinking that somebody might have put oleander in two of Laurence's capsules. Maybe Laurence gave Libby one of them. She didn't die

24

"I did know who that girl in L.A. was…"

until four days after Laurence, but that's not hard to explain. She may not have needed a capsule until then. Maybe she needed one that day because the air pollution was especially bad and she was feeling ill."

"I never knew exactly when she died," Charlie said. "But Laurence was in L.A. about ten days before *he* died. Maybe he gave Libby the capsules then."

"That's interesting," I said. "I'm going to Los Angeles myself soon. Maybe I'll find out something there."

He looked at his watch. "I have to go," he said.

I got up and walked to the door with him. I was sorry that he was leaving. At the door, he turned towards me. He looked at me for a little longer than he needed to.

"Goodbye," he said.

4

Charlotte Mercer

When I stopped in front of K9 Korners at 6 p.m., Gwen was locking the front door.

"Do you know the Palm Garden Restaurant?" she asked me.

"Yes," I replied. "Do you want to ride there in my car?"

"No, I'll follow you in mine," she said.

Gwen got into her car—she had a bright yellow Saab. I followed her in my old cream VW and we drove back towards the town center. It took us only five minutes.

There are tables outside the Palm Garden Restaurant.

We sat at a small one and we ordered drinks. We talked for a while about unimportant things. Then I said, "I've spoken with Charlie Scorsoni. Is he on your list?"

"My list of people who might have killed Laurence?" she said. "No, I don't think so."

She took a piece of paper and a pen out of her bag.

"This is where you can find Greg and Diane, if you still want to talk to them," she said. She wrote down their names, addresses and phone numbers.

"Thanks," I said. "Neither of them has written or spoken to Nikki since she got out of jail."

"That's sad," she replied. "Nikki was very good to them."

"What do *you* think of Nikki?" I asked her.

"I'm not really sure," she replied. "I hated her when Laurence divorced me, but I'd like to talk to her now. We might understand each other a lot better." She looked at me for a moment, then she went on. "I had an affair when I was about thirty. The affair only lasted for six weeks, but it was the best six weeks of my life. I kept it a secret for as long as I could, but then Laurence began to have suspicions. In the end, I told him about my lover. That was a mistake. That was when Laurence decided to divorce me."

"Where's the man now?" I asked.

"My lover?" she said. Suddenly, she was angry. "Why do you ask? He didn't kill Laurence! Don't try to blame somebody who had nothing to do with it!"

"OK," I said. "I can't *make* you tell me who he is—"

"That's right," she said quickly. "And you won't find out from anybody else."

We sat silently for the next few minutes. I watched her calm down[25], then I said, "Let's talk again about Laurence

27

and the other women."

She laughed a little, shaking her head. "I'm sorry, Kinsey. I didn't mean to get angry," she said.

"It's OK," I said. "But please tell me—who hated Laurence enough to kill him?"

"I've thought about that all afternoon, and I'm not sure about the answer. Divorce attorneys are never very popular, but most of them don't get murdered."

"Laurence had several affairs while he was married to Nikki. Perhaps one of his lovers killed him?"

"He did have a dangerous affair once, with the wife of a Santa Teresa judge," Gwen said. "Charlotte Mercer was her name. She phoned me after he broke up with[26] her. She wanted to tell me about it!"

"Was that before or after your divorce?" I asked.

"She called me after the divorce. But I don't know when Laurence began his affair with her. Why don't you talk to her? She'll be able to give you the details."

"That's great!" I said. "I'll tell her that she's my number one suspect!"

Gwen laughed. "If she wants to know who sent you," she said, "then please tell her!"

———

After Gwen left the restaurant, I found Charlotte Mercer's address in the phone book[27]. She and Judge Mercer lived in a house in the hills above Santa Teresa.

The sun was just beginning to set when I got there. The house had a view of the sea, which looked wonderful under the pink-and-blue sky. A housekeeper opened the door, then she left me waiting in a wide, cool hallway.

"Yes, what do you want?" someone behind me said a few

minutes later.

I turned and saw a small woman with short blond hair, good legs, and lovely, smooth skin on her face. She must have been in her mid-fifties, but a good surgeon had been at work on her[28].

"I'm Kinsey Millhone," I said. "I'm a private detective. I'm investigating the death of Laurence Fife."

Her smile had been polite. Now it became cruel.

"I hope this won't take long," she said. "Come outside. I've left my drink there."

I followed her to the back of the house. There were some white chairs with green cushions. She sat down in one and picked up her drink from a small glass table.

"Who sent you here, Nikki or Gwen?" she asked. She looked away from me, towards the sea. She didn't seem to need an answer. "Sit down."

I chose a chair not far from hers. I could see a swimming pool beyond some small trees.

"I'll tell you something," she said. "I wasn't Laurence Fife's first lover and I wasn't his last, but I *was* the best."

"Is that why he broke up with you?" I said.

She laughed angrily.

"OK, Laurence broke up with me—it's true. In fact, he broke up with me twice! I'd had a long affair with him before he divorced Gwen, and he broke up with me when he married Nikki. But Laurence often fell in love with the same woman twice. Suddenly, he wanted to meet me again. We started another affair, a few months before he died. But then he broke up with me for the second time."

"Why? What happened that second time?"

"He'd started an affair with someone else," Charlotte said.

29

"Laurence and I started another affair, a few months before he died."

"He told me that, but he wouldn't tell me who it was. It was very secret—very exciting!"

"I'm surprised that you weren't a suspect when he was killed," I said.

"Me?" she said, laughing. "Charlotte Mercer—the wife of an important judge? I didn't even have to speak at Nikki's trial. And the police knew about my affairs with Laurence. But they already had a suspect from the moment that he died."

"That was Nikki?"

"Yes, Nikki. But I don't think that she killed anybody. She was too—nice!" Charlotte made the word sound horrible. "Nobody cared about what I thought," she continued.

"OK. Tell me about Gwen," I said.

"Gwen? Gwen was stupid. Another *nice* lady. I don't know why she stayed married to Laurence Fife for thirteen years. He was a cold, cruel man."

"What about Libby Glass? Did you ever hear about her?"

"No."

"Sharon Napier?"

"Oh, yes. I knew *her*. The first time that I ever saw that woman, I knew that something was wrong about her. And I soon found out what it was."

"Was Laurence having an affair with Sharon?" I asked.

"Oh no, no! The truth was better than that. He'd had an affair with her *mother*. I paid a private detective to find out about that. Laurence destroyed that woman's life. Her husband divorced her and she started to drink too much. She became an alcoholic. She was very ill. And Sharon knew about her mother's affair. One day, Sharon arrived at Laurence's office and made him give her a job. It was a kind

31

of blackmail[29]! But she was a terrible secretary. She wanted revenge[30], so she went to work every day and did what she wanted to do, and no more."

"Could *she* have killed Laurence?" I asked.

"Yes, she could have killed him."

Suddenly, Charlotte looked back at the house. "It's time for you to go now," she said. "My husband will be home in a minute. I don't want to explain to him why you're here."

"OK," I said. "Thanks. You've helped me a lot."

I left Charlotte Mercer sitting outside with her drink, and I walked around the side of the house, back to my car.

5

Grace and Raymond Glass

It took me several days to find Sharon Napier's address. First, I discovered that she'd moved to Nevada, so I phoned a private detective who worked in that state. I told him what information I needed, and he said that he'd call me back. When he did call back, he said that Sharon was probably in Las Vegas. She'd lived in Reno for a while, but she'd left the city suddenly. She still owed money to several people there.

Next, I called a friend of mine in Las Vegas and I told him who I was looking for. He said that he'd try to find out where Sharon was living. I told him that I was driving to Los Angeles early the next week. I gave him a phone number so that he could call me there.

The next day was Sunday, and I spent it shopping and

cleaning my apartment. On Monday morning, I wrote a report for Nikki about what I had discovered so far and sent it to her. At two o'clock in the afternoon, I was driving towards Los Angeles.

———

I drove to the Hacienda Motor Lodge. I always stay there when I'm in L.A. The manager of the motel[31] is a large woman named Arlette. I like her.

Arlette gave me room number two. She always gives me that room. I put my suitcase on the bed and took out my running clothes. I changed quickly, and I went for a short run. Then I returned to the motel, and had a shower. Next, I read through my notes and made some phone calls.

I wanted to find Lyle Abernathy, the boyfriend of Libby Glass. At the time of Libby's death, he had worked for the Wonder Bread Company. First, I called their number, but I wasn't surprised to discover that he had left the company years before. And the manager there didn't know where Lyle was living or working. Next, I checked the L.A. phone book. Lyle's name wasn't in it, but a man named Raymond Glass was listed. He lived in Sherman Oaks, a few miles from L.A. I checked the number with the notes that I'd made from the police investigation report. Yes, that was Libby's parents' address.

Then I phoned my friend in Las Vegas. He'd already learned something about Sharon Napier, but he needed another half-day to check the information.

After that, I called Nikki in Santa Teresa. I told her where I was and what I was doing. Next I called my answering service. Charlie Scorsoni had tried to call me, from Denver, but he hadn't left a message. I decided that if Charlie had important news for me, he'd call back. I gave the answering service the phone number of the Hacienda Motor Lodge.

Then, I went to a restaurant to eat dinner. After dinner, I returned to the motel and watched TV with Arlette.

———

The next morning, I drove over the mountain into the San Fernando Valley, and into the little town of Sherman Oaks. Libby Glass's parents lived in a small apartment building there. There were four apartments in the building.

When I rang the doorbell, the door of apartment number one was opened by a tired woman in her early fifties. She had large, dark eyes.

"Are you Mrs Glass?" I asked. "My name's Kinsey Millhone. I'm a private investigator. I work in Santa Teresa."

"Is this about Elizabeth?" she asked.

"Yes, it's about your daughter," I said. "Did you always call her Elizabeth—not Libby?"

"Oh, we never called her Libby," Mrs Glass said. "She called herself that. But her father and I didn't like it."

After a moment, the woman moved back into the living room. I followed her. Beyond the living room, there was a small dining room. Near the doorway to the dining room, I saw a heavy man in his sixties. He was sitting in a wheel-chair[32]. He looked at me, but he didn't speak. The woman went across to him and turned his chair towards a TV which stood in the corner of the room. Then she put headphones[33] over his ears and pressed a switch on the TV. Now *he* could hear the TV, but we couldn't.

"I'm Grace," she said to me. "That's Raymond, Elizabeth's father. He was injured in a car accident three years ago. He doesn't talk now, but he can hear. He gets upset if he hears anybody talking about Elizabeth. Would you like to see a picture of her?"

There was a photograph of Libby Glass on a table near the window. Grace looked at it herself for a moment before giving the photo to me. Libby had blond hair, cut short, blue eyes and a big wide smile.

"She was lovely," I said. "I believe that she worked as an accountant at Haycraft and McNiece in L.A. How long was she with that company?"

"About a year and a half," Grace said.

"What can you tell me about her boyfriend?" I asked. "Do you know where he is now?"

"Lyle? Oh, he'll be here soon. He comes every day at lunchtime. He helps me look after Raymond. Lyle's a good boy. He and Elizabeth had known each other in school. They started to study at Santa Monica City College together. But Lyle soon decided to leave college, and that's when the problems started."

"Was that when he went to work for Wonder Bread?"

"Oh no, Lyle's had many jobs," Grace replied. "At first, he was going to be a lawyer, but then he changed his mind[34]. He said that the law was too boring. When he left college, Elizabeth was very disappointed. She was living in her own apartment by then. Elizabeth wanted to do well. She wanted Lyle to do well too."

"Did they live together at her apartment?" I asked.

"No, they didn't," she replied. "Elizabeth said that she didn't want to live with Lyle. But I *wanted* them to live together. I thought that it would help their relationship. Raymond didn't agree with me. He thought that Elizabeth could find somebody better than Lyle."

35

Libby had blond hair, blue eyes and a big wide smile.

"And do you know why they ended their relationship?" I asked. "Was Elizabeth having an affair with somebody else?"

"You're talking about that attorney in Santa Teresa."

"Yes. It's his death that I'm investigating," I said. "Did Elizabeth ever talk to you about him?"

"No. I never knew anything about him until the police came from Santa Teresa to talk to us. But Elizabeth would never have fallen in love with a married man."

Suddenly, Grace began to cry. "Somebody murdered my daughter!" she said. "Why would anybody do that?"

"Could it have been an accident?" I asked. "She died from oleander poisoning. The attorney, Laurence Fife, died from oleander poisoning too. Someone put powdered oleander in one of his allergy capsules. Maybe they put oleander in more than one capsule. Maybe Fife and Elizabeth were working on some accounts together. Maybe she was feeling ill, and Fife gave her some of his capsules."

She stopped crying and thought about this for a moment, then she said, "But the police said that the attorney died several days *before* Elizabeth."

"Maybe she didn't take the capsule with the poison in it until three or four days after he gave it to her. *Did* Elizabeth have any allergies?"

Grace began to cry again. "No, I don't think so," she said. Then she looked at me. "I don't want to talk about this any more. But please stay for lunch and meet Lyle. Maybe he can tell you something that will help you."

6

Lyle Abernathy

Lyle Abernathy came into the apartment smiling. He was not much taller than me, and he was about my age. His hair was blond, and his eyes were pale blue. He kissed Grace on her cheek before he saw me. When he did see me, his smile disappeared.

"Lyle, this is Kinsey Millhone," Grace told him.

"Please call me Kinsey," I said, holding out my hand. "I'm a private investigator from Santa Teresa. I've been talking to Grace about her daughter." He looked worried. He shook my hand quickly, then turned away.

Lyle moved across the room to Raymond without looking at me. He took the headphones off the older man and turned off the TV. "How are you feeling today?" he asked him.

During lunch, Lyle said nothing to me and he spoke very little to Grace.

"What sort of work do you do, Lyle?" I asked him.

"Building," he said. He didn't want to talk to me, and he did nothing to hide that.

"I have to drive to Las Vegas today," I said to Grace. "But I'd like to visit you again on my way back to Santa Teresa. Do you still have any of Elizabeth's things here?"

Grace looked quickly at Lyle, but he was looking down at his food. "Yes," she said after a moment. "There are some big wooden boxes in the basement[35] of this building, aren't there, Lyle? Elizabeth's books and papers are in one of them."

Suddenly, Raymond made an angry sound—he'd heard Elizabeth's name. Lyle got up and pushed the old man's wheelchair out of the room.

"I'm sorry. I shouldn't have spoken about Elizabeth in front of Raymond," I said.

"Don't worry about it," Grace replied. "Come here again when you get back to L.A. You can look at Elizabeth's things then. I'm sure that it will be all right."

I left the apartment soon after that and I waited in my car across the street. I could see Lyle's truck parked outside the building. A few minutes later, he came out. He saw my car and smiled to himself, then he got into the truck and drove away fast. I followed.

Lyle was working at a house not far away. He got out of his truck and walked around the side of the building. I parked my car in the street and followed him again. He had already started to work at the back of the house when I got there.

"I don't want to talk to you," he said.

I smiled. "Well, you don't have to tell me anything, Lyle," I said. "I can spend this afternoon finding out all about you. I can do it with six phone calls from a motel room."

"Do it," he said. "I've got nothing to hide[36]."

"Then why won't you talk to me?" I said. "Please tell me why you broke up with Libby."

"She broke up with *me*, after she met that attorney from Santa Teresa," he replied.

"Laurence Fife?" I said.

"I never knew his name. She wouldn't tell me anything about him. At first, they were just having meetings about business—she worked on his accounts. He came to L.A. a few times and they went out for dinner. Then she fell in love with him. That's all that I know about him."

"OK, Lyle. Who do *you* think killed Libby?"

He looked at me carefully with his pale blue eyes.

39

For a few moments, he didn't speak. Then he answered me sadly. "Maybe she killed herself," he said. "She loved the attorney very much."

"Did she really love him enough to kill herself when he died?" I asked.

"I don't know. Perhaps she did."

"How did she find out about Fife's death?" I asked.

"Someone called her from Santa Teresa and told her about it."

"How do *you* know that?"

"Because she phoned me that day. She was very unhappy about something. I went to see her—she asked me to come. But when I got to her apartment, she didn't want to talk to me after all. She told me about the attorney's death, but she didn't want me to stay with her, so I left. And the next thing that I heard was that she was dead."

"Who found Libby's body?" I asked.

"The manager of the apartment building where she lived," he replied. "Libby didn't go to work for a few days, and she didn't phone anybody. Her boss at Haycraft and McNiece got worried and he went to her apartment. When the manager of the building opened the door, he found Libby dead on her bathroom floor. By then, she'd been dead for several days."

"Did Libby have any allergies, Lyle? Or was she ill in any way when you last saw her?"

"I don't remember. I last saw her just after she heard the news about the attorney's death. That was a Wednesday. The police said that she died on the next Saturday night."

"OK. Do you know if the attorney kept anything at her apartment? Did he keep any medicines there? Maybe Libby took something that was meant to kill *him*."

"I don't know!" he shouted. He was getting angry now.

I tore a page out of my notebook and wrote down the phone number of the motel. I gave it to Lyle.

"Please call me if you think of anything that might help me," I said. "Leave a message if I'm not at the motel."

He pushed the piece of paper into his shirt pocket.

"I'll be back in Los Angeles at the end of the week," I said. "Maybe I'll come and see you again."

I walked back to my car. I didn't think that Lyle had told me the whole truth, but I couldn't be sure.

7

Sharon Napier

Next, I visited Haycraft and McNiece, the business management company where Libby had worked. The offices were in Westwood, not far from my motel.

"Can I talk to a senior accountant?" I asked the receptionist. I gave the girl one of my business cards[37] and she looked at it without interest.

"I'm investigating the murder of a girl who used to work here," I went on.

"Oh yes, I heard about her," she said. "Mr McNiece isn't in the office today."

"Is Mr Haycraft here?"

"He died years ago," she said. "The person who you need to talk to is Garry Steinberg."

"That's great!" I said. "Can you ask him if I can talk to

him for a few minutes?"

"No. He's in New York for a few days."

This girl was not trying to be helpful. But I wasn't going to get angry!

"Is there anybody else here who might remember Libby Glass?" I asked her calmly.

"No," she said. "I'm sorry." She sounded very bored now, and she gave me back my business card.

I turned the card over and I wrote my motel phone number and the number of my answering service on the back.

"Please give this to Garry Steinberg when he gets back from New York," I said.

———

I went back to the motel and I made some phone calls. Ruth, Charlie Scorsoni's secretary, told me that Charlie was still in Denver. She gave me his hotel phone number. I called the hotel, but Charlie wasn't in, so I left my number with the receptionist. Then I called Nikki and told her what I had discovered that day. I told her that there were some papers in the basement of the Glasses' apartment building which I wanted to look at. And after that, I called my answering service. There were no messages for me.

My investigation didn't seem to be moving forward, so I put on my running clothes and drove to the beach.

———

An hour later, when I got back the motel, the phone was ringing in my room. It was my friend in Las Vegas. He now had Sharon Napier's home address.

"And she's working in the Fremont Casino[38], at one of the gambling tables," he said. "I heard that she's cheating. She could be in big trouble. In Las Vegas, nobody cares what you do, as long as you don't cheat."

"Thanks for the information," I said.

I went out to eat. And for the second time, the phone was ringing when I got back to my room. This time, it was Charlie Scorsoni.

"How's Denver?" I asked him.

"OK," he said. "How's L.A.?"

"It's OK too," I said. "But I'm driving to Las Vegas tonight. I now know where to find Sharon Napier."

"That's great," he said. "When you see her, tell her to pay me my six hundred dollars. When will you be back in Santa Teresa?"

"Maybe on Saturday. When I come back through Los Angeles on Friday, I'm going to look at some papers that belonged to Libby Glass. They're in a basement at her parents' apartment building in Sherman Oaks. But it won't take me long to look through the papers."

"I'm leaving Denver the day after tomorrow," Charlie said. "So I'll be back in Santa Teresa before you. Will you call me when you get back?"

"OK," I said, after a moment.

I put down the phone. The smile stayed on my face for several minutes.

Las Vegas is a six-hour drive from Los Angeles, and it was after midnight when I arrived there. I stopped at the first motel that I saw. It was called the Bagdad.

———

When I woke the next morning, I was starting to get a headache. I didn't feel well, and I hoped that I wasn't getting the flu[39]. I took a shower, got dressed, and went to my car. I drove to the address that my friend had given me. Sharon

Napier lived in an apartment on the other side of town. It was a first floor apartment in a building next to a swimming pool.

I looked through the front window of Sharon's apartment. The drapes[40] weren't quite pulled together. Between them, I could see a living room. I saw a table with two chairs. On one corner of the table, a phone was standing on top of a pile of papers.

After a minute, I walked around to the back of the building. Sharon's apartment number was painted on the rear door. Her kitchen drapes were pulled completely together, so I couldn't see into the room. But I was sure that Sharon wasn't at home.

I went back to the street, got into my car and drove to the Fremont Casino. Sharon Napier was working at one of the gambling tables. She was tall, with blond hair. I sat at another table and watched her for a while. Three men were playing cards[41] at her table. Sharon dealt the cards. The men played in complete silence.

At 1:30 p.m. another girl took Sharon's place at the table and Sharon walked across the casino to the coffee shop. I followed her. She sat down, ordered a cola, and lit a cigarette.

"Hi! Are you Sharon Napier?" I asked her. "I'm Kinsey Millhone. Can I sit down?"

She pointed with her cigarette to a chair near hers.

"I'm investigating the death of Laurence Fife," I said.

For a second or two, she didn't move. Then she said, "He was not a nice man." She began to smoke her cigarette.

"Did you work for him for long?" I asked.

She smiled. "You've already been asking questions and getting answers. So I expect that you already know the

Sharon dealt the cards. The men played in complete silence.

answer to that question."

"There's a lot that I don't know," I said. "What was it like to work for him? How did you feel about his death?"

"I felt really happy about his death," she replied. "I hated him, and I hated working as his secretary. Tell me something, Kinsey—who sent you here?"

"I'm working for Nikki Fife," I said, after a moment.

Sharon seemed surprised. "She's still in jail, isn't she?"

I shook my head. "No. She got out last week."

Sharon took a minute to think, then said, "I finish working here at seven o'clock. Why don't you come to my apartment after that? We can talk more privately there."

She told me her address and I didn't tell her that I already knew it. Then suddenly, she looked away to her left and moved her hand quickly. At first, I thought that she was lifting a hand to wave at a friend. She'd started to smile. But then she looked back at me. Quickly, she stood up and walked in front of me so that I couldn't see who she had been looking at.

"I've got to go back to my table now," she said. "That was my boss."

I was sure that this was a lie.

"OK. I'll see you after seven o'clock," I said.

"Come at 7:45," she replied.

I wrote my name, and the name of my motel, on a piece of paper from my notebook. Sharon put the note into her cigarette packet, then she walked away without looking back at me, or saying goodbye.

It was still early afternoon when I drove back to the Bagdad. My headache was worse now, and my body was aching too. I felt very cold. I *was* getting the flu.

At the motel, I got into bed without undressing and I tried to sleep. It was a long time before I got warm.

———

The sound of the phone ringing woke me. The room was dark. I switched on the light and picked up the phone.

"Hello?" I said.

"This is Sharon Napier. Did you forget about our meeting?"

I looked at my watch. It was 8:30 p.m. "I felt ill and I fell asleep!" I said. "I'm sorry! Can I come over now?"

"OK," she said. "Oh, wait a minute. There's somebody ringing my doorbell."

I couldn't believe that I had slept for so long! But as I waited for Sharon to return to the phone, I thought that my headache was a little better. I listened, and I heard Sharon open her door, and then I heard a small explosion[42].

A minute later, somebody picked up Sharon's phone. I expected to hear her voice and I nearly said her name. But then I heard the sound of somebody breathing, and a voice whispered, "Hello". It wasn't Sharon Napier's voice! Next came a little laugh, before the person in Sharon's apartment hung up[43].

Suddenly, I knew what the explosion had been! I got out of bed, picked up my jacket, left the motel and ran to my car.

I drove fast to Sharon's apartment building and parked across the street. Everything was quiet. Nobody was moving about. There were no crowds in the street, and there were no police cars. There were lights on in nearly every apartment, but Sharon's living room was in darkness.

I took a flashlight and a pair of rubber gloves[44] from my briefcase[45] on the back seat of the car. My hand touched the

47

small gun inside the case and I wanted to take it with me. But I wasn't sure what I was going to find in Sharon's apartment, or who might be waiting for me there. Had one of her neighbors heard the sound that I'd heard—the sound of a gun? If someone had heard the gunshot, the police might be inside the apartment already. Or they might come soon. And if Sharon was dead, meeting the police with a gun in my hand would not be good for me. So I left my gun in the briefcase and got out of the car.

Sharon's front door was locked. I rang the doorbell and called "Sharon?" softly. No answer! I pulled on my rubber gloves and I went quietly round to the back of the building.

Sharon's rear door was locked too, and all the rooms in her apartment were in darkness. I knocked on the window and said, "Sharon?" again. Everything was quiet. I looked around me. If there was an extra door key, it would be hidden somewhere nearby. There was a low wall around the small back garden. A large pot of flowers stood against the wall. I lifted the pot—and I found a key!

I unlocked the rear door and opened it an inch or two. "Sharon!" I whispered. I held the flashlight above my head, ready to hit anybody who attacked me, then I put my other hand inside the room. I felt the wall, found a light switch and pushed it down. The kitchen light came on. I listened for a minute, but there were no sounds in the apartment.

I entered the kitchen. There was nobody in it. Then I looked into the living room. I turned on my flashlight there. I didn't want anybody in the street to see the lights at the front of Sharon's apartment come on.

I saw Sharon Napier lying on the floor. She was wearing a pretty green bathrobe[46]. She was either dead or asleep.

Moving quickly but carefully, I searched the bedroom and the bathroom. There was nobody in either of them. Finally, I went back to Sharon and knelt on the floor beside her.

Sharon wasn't asleep. She was dead. There was a bullet hole in her neck and there was some blood on the carpet under her head. Her eyes were open. I wanted to tell her that I was sorry for being too late.

Now I had a problem. I had to tell somebody about Sharon. But I didn't want to answer questions from the Las Vegas police. So I spoke carefully when I phoned them.

"Hello," I said. "I heard some strange noises in my neighbor's apartment and now she won't come to her door. I'm worried about her. Maybe she's hurt."

The officer who I spoke to sounded bored. But he took Sharon's address and said that he'd send someone. When he asked for my name, I hung up.

I looked quickly at the pile of papers under Sharon's phone. Most of them were bills[47]. I picked them up and put them in my pocket—maybe I'd learn something from them later. Then I looked back at Sharon. Who'd killed her? Was it somebody from the casino—somebody who'd discovered that she'd been cheating? Or did she know something about Laurence Fife—something that somebody else didn't want her to tell me?

The police would be arriving soon. It was time to get out of the apartment. I stepped over Sharon, then I remembered something and I stopped. At the coffee shop, she'd taken the piece of paper with my name and motel phone number written on it. She'd put it inside her cigarette packet. But where was it now? I looked around quickly. The paper wasn't on the table in the living room. I went into the bathroom, then the bedroom, and the kitchen. No piece of paper, and no cigarette packet! I went back to the living room and looked down at Sharon again. There were two large pockets on the green bathrobe that she was wearing.

I found the cigarette packet in one of the pockets. The piece of paper was still inside it. I put the paper in one of the pockets of my jacket, then I turned out the kitchen light, turned off my flashlight, and left the apartment by the rear door. I put the key back under the pot of flowers and walked around to the front of the building.

A police car had stopped in the street, outside the apartments. I walked slowly past it.

Inside my car, I pulled off the rubber gloves. My hands were shaking and I felt sick. I drove away as an officer got out of the police car and started to walk towards the back of Sharon's apartment. He had his hand on his gun.

At the Bagdad Motel, I paid my bill and packed my bag. In a few minutes, I was leaving Las Vegas, driving down Highway 93, going south-east. At Boulder City, I drove onto Highway 95, and headed south. After another hour, I found a cheap motel, where I slept for ten hours.

8

Greg and Diane Fife

In the morning, I drove back into California, to Salton Sea—the huge lake south-east of Palm Springs. I found Greg Fife easily. He was living in a little gray trailer[48], near the eastern shore[49] of the lake. He invited me inside.

Greg was twenty-five, but he looked younger than that. He also looked a lot like his father, Laurence.

"Can I talk to you about your father?" I asked.

"Did you know him?"

"I worked for him a few times," I replied. "But I didn't know him well. I've heard that he wasn't a nice man."

"Have you?" he said.

"How did you feel about Nikki?" I asked.

"Not very good," he replied.

Sometimes I get tired of [50] trying to get information from people who don't want to give it to me.

"Why don't we go outside?" I said.

"Why?" he asked.

"Why do you think?" I said angrily. "Because I might get some better answers from the lake!"

I opened the door.

Greg laughed suddenly, and he followed me out of the trailer. I pulled off my shoes and we walked along the shore.

"What do you remember about the time just before your father died?" I asked. "I'm trying to find out what happened in the weeks before his death."

"We came here for a weekend just before his death," he replied sadly. "It was September. I was happy that weekend, it was a good time. That's one reason why I came here to live."

I pulled off my shoes and we walked along the shore.

"What do you remember about that weekend?" I asked.

"I was seventeen, then," Greg replied. "God, I was stupid! I thought that my father was wonderful."

"Did the two of you come here alone that weekend?"

"Oh, no, Nikki and Colin came too. Diane was ill and she stayed in Santa Teresa, at Mom's house."

"How did you feel about Colin then?" I asked carefully.

"I liked him. And I felt sorry for him. But I didn't understand why we had to do everything that Colin wanted to do. I needed Dad's love, too."

"Greg, did your father ever talk to you about his lovers?" I asked him.

"Dad never talked to me about anything," Greg replied. "Listen, can we stop talking about this for a few minutes?"

I smiled at Greg and I started to run along the beach. "Do you run?" I shouted back to him.

He was soon by my side, and we ran together without speaking. But I was thinking. Sharon Napier knew something that she didn't live long enough to tell me. What was it? Nothing that had happened eight years before was making sense[51] to me—not Laurence Fife's death, not Libby Glass's death. But what about Sharon Napier's death, the day before? I could think of a reason for that. Sharon *had* made sense of those other deaths and she had been blackmailing someone. She had been blackmailing a killer!

I stopped running. "I have to go now, Greg," I said, "I want to get to Claremont before night. I want to talk to Diane. Do you have any messages for her?"

"She knows where I am," he said. "We talk sometimes."

"One more thing. What do you remember about your father's allergies?" I asked him.

53

"He was allergic to lots of things, especially to dogs and cats," Greg replied.

"Did he have any allergy capsules with him when the family came down here that weekend?"

"I don't remember. But my guess is that he didn't bring any capsules here. The air down here is very good. And the dog wasn't with us—we left him at home in Montebello. So my father wouldn't have needed his medicines."

"Bruno got killed, didn't he?"

"Yes, Bruno got killed in an accident," Greg said. "In fact, he was killed that weekend, while we were here."

That was interesting. Who had been at the house in Montebello that weekend? Who had let the dog out of the house? The housekeeper? Somebody else?

"How did you find out about Bruno?" I asked.

"We found out about the accident when we got home," he said. "Mom had taken Diane over to Dad's house to get something. They found Bruno, at the side of the road, near the house. He'd been dead for some time."

"How did you feel about Mrs Voss, your father's housekeeper?" I asked him. "What was she like?"

"Oh, she was OK," Greg replied. "I'm sorry, but I don't know anything else that might help you."

"Thanks, Greg," I said. "I may need to talk to you again."

———

I got to Claremont at six o'clock that evening, and I slept at the house of some friends who live there. The next day, I met Diane Fife for lunch at a restaurant. Greg had phoned her and told her about my visit with him.

"Is Colin back at home with Nikki?" she asked me. "I'd like to see him."

"Nikki was on her way to get him from Monterey when I talked to her a couple of days ago," I said.

"Did you meet Mom?"

"Yes. I liked Gwen a lot."

Diane smiled. "I think that Dad was really stupid to divorce her and marry Nikki. He didn't love Nikki. I don't think that he ever loved anybody in his life—except Colin."

We ate silently for a minute or two. Then I said, "Greg told me that you missed that weekend trip to Salton Sea."

"The September trip, just before Dad died? Yes, I did. I *did* miss that trip. I had the flu. So I stayed in Santa Teresa, with Mom."

"How did the dog get out of the house?" I asked.

She looked down at her hands. "What dog?"

"Bruno," I said. "Greg said that Bruno got hit by a car that weekend. Who let him out of the house? Was Mrs Voss staying there while the family was away?"

Diane looked at me quickly but carefully. Then she looked away again. "No, I don't think so," she said. Her face went red. She looked at the clock on the wall behind me.

"I've got a class to go to," she said suddenly.

"Are you OK, Diane?" I asked.

"Yes, I'm fine," she said. She picked up her bag and some books. "Oh, I nearly forgot—I've got something for Colin."

She gave me a paper bag. "Will you give him this, if you see him? I had some family photographs. I've put them into an album[52] for him."

She stood up. "I'm sorry, I don't have any more time to talk," she said.

"Can I drive you somewhere?" I asked her.

"No. I've got a car," she said. She seemed upset.

"Diane, what's wrong?" I said.

She sat down again. When she spoke, her voice was quiet and very sad.

"I was thinking about Bruno," she whispered. "I let him out of the house myself. It was the day when the others left to go to Salton Sea. Nikki told me to let Bruno have a run outside before Mom came to get me. So I let him out of the house. But I was feeling ill that weekend. I had the flu. I forgot about the dog when Mom arrived. I forgot to put him back inside. Bruno was outside for two days before I remembered about him. I felt terrible when I did remember. That's why Mom and I drove over to Montebello again. We went to give Bruno some food and put him back into the house."

She was crying now. "Bruno got killed because I forgot about him. I've never told anybody about that. Only Mom knows. You won't tell anybody about it now, will you? Nikki would hate me."

"Nikki's not going to hate you because the dog got killed, Diane," I said. "That was eight years ago. Why does it matter so much?"

"Because I think that someone got into the house while the dog was out," she said. "Someone got into the house and changed Dad's medicine. And that's why he died!"

She started to cry more loudly, and two men at another table looked across at us.

"Let's get out of here," I said. I picked up Diane's books and her bag, and I left some money to pay the bill. Then I held her arm and helped her to the door. By the time we got outside, she had calmed down.

"I'm sorry," she said.

"It's OK, Diane," I said. "I'm sorry that I upset you."

56

"I thought that you must know the truth about Bruno," she said. "When you asked that question, I thought that you must have found out about it. I've felt terrible about Bruno's death for so long."

"If someone had wanted to get into the house, he would have let the dog out himself," I said. "Or he would have killed Bruno, and made the death look like an accident."

"Maybe," she replied. "Yes, maybe you're right."

"Listen Diane, why don't you forget about your classes today and go home?"

"Maybe I'll do that," she said.

9

Garry Steinberg

When I got back to Los Angeles, I drove straight to the Hacienda Motor Lodge. I went into the manager's office to check for messages. Arlette had four for me. Three were from Charlie Scorsoni. The fourth was from the receptionist at Haycraft and McNiece.

"Mr Scorsoni called from Denver, Colorado, then from Tucson, Arizona. Last night he called from Santa Teresa," Arlette said. "He sounded nice. Oh, and I gave your phone number in Las Vegas to two people who didn't want to leave messages. I hope that's OK."

"Yes, that's OK," I said. "Do you have any idea who these people were?"

"One was male, one was female," Arlette told me. "They

didn't give me their names."

When I got to my room, I pulled off my shoes and I called Charlie Scorsoni's office in Santa Teresa. He wasn't there. Then I called the receptionist at Haycraft and McNiece. She told me that Garry Steinberg was back from New York and he could talk to me that afternoon. I told her that I'd be there in an hour. Then I called Grace Glass and told her that I'd be coming to see her in the evening.

The next call was one that I didn't want to make, but I made it. It was to my friend in Las Vegas.

"Kinsey!" he said. "I tried to speak to you earlier. Why do you always make trouble for me? I gave you some information about Sharon Napier, and now I've heard that she's dead. And she's dead because somebody shot her!"

"We don't *know* that she was shot because of me!"

"No, but somebody will remember that I was asking questions about her at the Fremont Casino. And then she was found with a bullet hole in her neck!"

I told my friend that I was very sorry and I asked him to let me know about anything new that he found out.

———

Garry Steinberg was a very nice man. He had dark hair and dark eyes. I guessed that he was in his early thirties.

"Why do you want to know about Libby Glass?" he asked.

I explained about my investigation. He listened carefully, then said, "What can I tell you?"

"How long had Laurence Fife been a client of your company?" I asked him.

"This company looked after Fife's personal accounts first, for about a year. But his law firm—Fife and Scorsoni—had only been our clients for six months when Libby died. We'd just got our new computer then, and Libby was putting all our clients' accounts onto the computer. She was a very good accountant."

"So she did more work for Laurence Fife than for Charlie Scorsoni?"

"At first, yes. After that, she did about the same amount for each of them."

"What happened to Laurence Fife's money after he died? Do you know?" I asked.

"Yes. He left it all to his three kids," he replied.

"And does Haycraft and McNiece work for Scorsoni and Powers?"

"No," Garry said. "Charlie Scorsoni gave the work to another company after Fife's death. But I met Scorsoni a few times. He seemed to be a nice guy."

"Can I look at the Fife and Scorsoni accounts, Garry?"

"No, I'm sorry," he answered. "I can't show them to you without Scorsoni's permission."

"OK," I said. "Tell me more about Libby Glass. Do you think that she was having an affair with Laurence Fife?"

Garry laughed. "I don't know about that. I knew that she'd broken up with Lyle Abernathy. And I did meet *him*. He came here wanting a job once, but he didn't get one. I didn't like him."

"Do you still have Abernathy's job application[53] here, Garry?" I asked. Suddenly I began to feel a little excited.

"It's possible. I'll try to find it later," Garry said. "And maybe I'll find the old Fife and Scorsoni accounts too. I can look at them myself, of course. But now I'll try to answer your question about Libby. My guess is that she *wasn't* having an affair with Laurence Fife."

59

He looked at his watch. "I have to meet someone in a minute or two."

I stood up and shook his hand across the desk. I was feeling good, though I didn't really know why.

"Thanks, Garry," I said.

————

I got back to my motel room and spent two hours writing notes about the case. Then I went for a run, returned to my room and took a shower. Next I had something to eat. When I'd finished it was 6:45 p.m., so I drove over the mountain to Sherman Oaks.

Mrs Glass opened the door of her apartment and we went into the living room. Her husband wasn't there.

"Raymond had a bad day," Grace explained. "Lyle came here on his way home from work, and we helped Raymond get into bed."

We talked for half an hour, then I asked about Libby's papers.

"Elizabeth's things are in the basement of this building," Grace said. "I'll get my key."

She left the room and returned a moment later with a key. I followed her out of the apartment, and across the hallway to the door of the basement stairs. The door was locked, and Grace opened it with her key. She switched on a light which shone onto the stairs. As we went down them, I could see some big wooden boxes on the floor below.

Suddenly, I knew that something wasn't right! But before I could decide what was wrong, there was an explosion and then the stairs were in darkness. Someone had shot at the light above us. Grace screamed and I pulled her quickly back up the stairs, to the hallway.

At the same time, I heard someone running up some other stairs. I quickly realized that there was another entrance to the basement—some steps which led down from outside the building. Someone had come in that way, and now they were leaving that way too.

I left Grace and I ran through the hallway, out of the building, and towards the other entrance to the basement. But it was dark outside, and I couldn't see anybody. A moment later, I heard a car start in the next street, then I heard it drive away fast. I knew that I was too late again!

I ran back to my car and got my flashlight and my gun. I didn't think that there was anybody still in the basement, but I was tired of being surprised. I went back into the building.

Grace was sitting on the hallway floor, by the basement door. She was crying. I helped her to stand up.

"Lyle knew that I was coming to look at Libby's things tonight, didn't he, Grace?" I said.

"That wasn't Lyle," she said. "He's a good boy. He wouldn't frighten me like that."

I took her back into her apartment and I made her sit down. Then I returned to the basement door. I turned on my flashlight. I walked carefully down the stairs and I looked around me.

I quickly guessed which of the wooden boxes belonged to Mrs Glass, because it was broken open. Six smaller boxes, made of cardboard, had been taken out of it. All of them had the name "Elizabeth" written on the side, and all of them had been broken open too. Everything in the boxes had been thrown onto the floor. Who'd done this? Had they found what they were looking for?

A moment later, I heard Grace coming down into the

basement. "Elizabeth's things!" she whispered, when she saw the boxes.

Her face was pale, but she'd stopped crying. She started looking through the papers, books, magazines and clothes, toys and games. And I began putting the things back into the cardboard boxes.

"Can I take these things and look through them tonight, Grace?" I asked. "I'll bring them back to you in the morning."

I didn't really expect to find anything interesting, but I would have to look. Lyle Abernathy couldn't have been in the basement for very long. He might not have found what he was looking for. But *had* it been Lyle in the basement? Suddenly, I had doubts. Lyle knew that I was coming back to look at Libby's things. So why hadn't he searched the boxes during the three days since my first visit?

Grace helped me to carry the cardboard boxes to my car. There were six of them.

"I'll be back early tomorrow morning," I told her.

———

It was four o'clock in the morning when I finished looking through the last box of school papers, letters, bills, clothes and books. But none of these things had helped me with my investigation. If there had ever been any useful information, it was gone now. This was the second time that I'd arrived somewhere too late, and it made me angry. I began to put the things back into the box.

Then a letter fell out from between the pages of a book that I was holding. There was no date on the letter and there was no envelope with it. I picked it up by one corner—I didn't want to put my own fingerprints on it—and read it.

I began putting the things back into the cardboard boxes.

Darling Elizabeth,

I know that you find life difficult when we are not together. You are much more honest about your feelings than I am. I do love you, and I want you to know that. But I have my wife, my kids, and my work. It would be wrong for me to leave all of them now. Our love is important to me too, but I can't decide anything about my future yet. Please believe me, Elizabeth.

Laurence.

The letter seemed to prove that there had been an affair between Libby and Laurence. But I didn't believe it! Maybe I didn't want to believe it. I was worried about the name "Elizabeth". Everybody except her parents had called Grace and Raymond's daughter, "Libby". And was the letter really from Laurence Fife? Well, there were ways to check that. I found a large envelope and I carefully put the letter into it.

Then I lay on the bed and began to think about everything that had happened that week. Had Sharon Napier discovered that Libby and Laurence had had an affair? Was that what she was going to tell me the night that she died?

"No, not if she was going to blackmail somebody with that information!" I thought.

But had she *already* blackmailed somebody with the information? And was *that* why she was killed? Yes, that had to be the reason! Someone had followed me to Las Vegas. This person knew that I would talk to Sharon Napier. This person knew that Sharon could tell me something about the Fife and Glass murders. I couldn't prove this. But if I was getting close to the truth, there was danger for me too. Why?

"Because a killer is now very worried," I thought. "For eight years, the killer has been safe. Nobody has asked any new questions about the murders. But now the investigation is beginning again."

Suddenly, I started to think about Nikki Fife in a new way. For eight years, I had believed that Nikki was innocent. I'd never believed that she'd killed Laurence. And when Dolan didn't agree with me, I'd said, "If she killed Libby, why would she want a new investigation?"

But maybe Nikki wasn't innocent. Maybe the person that Sharon had been blackmailing was Nikki. Did Sharon know something that connected Nikki to Libby's death? If there was a connection, maybe Nikki had paid me to investigate Laurence's death because I would have to talk to Sharon. Maybe Nikki hadn't known where Sharon was living. Maybe she'd used me to find out. Maybe she'd followed me to Las Vegas and killed Sharon that Wednesday evening. And then she could have followed me back to Sherman Oaks and broken into the Glasses' basement while I was in her apartment. And how did Nikki know about Libby's papers? Because I'd told her about them when I'd phoned her!

I went on thinking about Nikki. Why would she want to see Libby's papers? There was an answer to that question too! If there was anything in the papers which proved that Nikki had known about an affair between Libby and her husband, I would have to tell Lieutenant Dolan about it. Then maybe Nikki would be jailed again, this time for the murder of Libby Glass!

Now I was very worried. Was I working for someone who had killed three people? Had I helped Nikki with the third murder? Had I led her to the victim[54]—Sharon Napier?

10

Colin Fife

I left the motel early the next morning and I took the boxes of Libby's things back to the Glasses' apartment in Sherman Oaks.

"Did you find anything useful?" Grace asked me.

"No," I said. "If there ever was anything useful, someone else found it first." I didn't tell Grace about the letter.

After I put the boxes back in the basement, I said goodbye to the Glasses, and I drove home to Santa Teresa. I slept for a few hours, but at four o'clock I decided to visit Nikki.

The night before, I'd been worried about talking to Nikki. But now I was calm again. Was Nikki really a killer? No, I didn't think so. But if she *had* killed Sharon Napier, then she already knew everything that I'd discovered. If I started lying to Nikki now, she would guess that I suspected her. I would be in danger. Whatever the truth was about Nikki, I had to talk to her.

I drove to the beach house and I took Diane's photo album with me.

Nikki's smile was friendly when she said hello. "What's this?" she asked, when I showed her the album.

"Diane sent it for Colin," I said.

"That was kind of her," she said. "Come and see him. We're making bread together."

I followed her through the house to the kitchen. Colin was working at the table. Nikki put her hand on his arm. He turned quickly to look at me. His eyes were large and green, and his hair was the same color as Nikki's. He was a beautiful boy.

"I've told him that you were my first friend after I got out of jail," Nikki said. "It's so good to have him here."

Nikki opened a bottle of wine and we took our glasses outside and looked at the sea. I told Nikki about everything that had happened during the last few days. I told her about Sharon Napier's death and about my talks with Greg and Diane. And I told her about the letter that I'd found in Libby Glass's things.

"Would you recognize Laurence's handwriting?" I asked.

"Yes," she said.

I took the envelope out of my bag and carefully removed the letter. I held it by one corner while Nikki read it.

"Yes, that's his writing," she said. "Did Laurence send this to Libby Glass? I'm surprised that the affair was so serious. The others weren't."

At that moment, Colin came outside with the photo album. He put his finger on one of the pictures and said something which I couldn't understand.

"That's Diane and Greg, and their mother," Nikki said to him, speaking and moving her fingers at the same time.

He moved his own fingers to reply. "No Colin, *that's* Grandmother," Nikki said, turning to a picture on the previous page and pointing at it. "The other lady is *Diane's* mother. Grandmother Fife didn't look like that. Don't you remember her?"

Suddenly she smiled. "Oh no, how could he remember her?" she said to me. "Laurence's mother died when Colin was a year old."

Colin said something else to Nikki.

She looked at me again. "This is strange, Kinsey. He believes that Gwen is 'Daddy's mother'. I wonder why?"

She turned back to her son. "We'll look at this together later," she said. "Take it inside now, Colin."

We watched him go back inside the house.

"I've got to go now, Nikki," I said.

Nikki walked with me to the front door. I got into my car and sat for a moment, thinking about Colin's mistake about Gwen. It was strange. Very strange!

———

When I got back to my apartment, Charlie Scorsoni was waiting outside. I wasn't ready for his visit. I needed to have a shower, change my clothes and brush my hair before he saw me. But it was too late for that.

"You always meet me at a bad time," I said.

He smiled. "Have a shower. Get dressed. Then we'll go out to eat."

I did what he asked, and we drove in my car to an expensive restaurant. While we were waiting for the food, Charlie asked about my investigation.

"I don't want to talk about it," I said. "It's not going well." Suddenly, I asked, "Have you ever been married, Charlie?"

"No," he answered. "I've never had time for marriage. I work, and that's the only thing that interests me."

I smiled. I understood his feelings. Since my second divorce, there hadn't been many men in my life. I'd only wanted to work. I loved my job, so that wasn't a problem for me. But I realized that at that moment, being with Charlie was more interesting than work.

We ate our meal, and Charlie talked about his years at law school and about his family. His father had been an alcoholic. He'd spent all his money on drink. Then he'd become very ill. After his death, it had taken Charlie several years to pay

...being with Charlie was more interesting than work.

his father's hospital bills.

When we'd finished our coffee, we left the restaurant and walked back to my car. This time, Charlie drove the VW. He drove with one hand, and he put his other hand over mine.

"Guess what we're going to do next?" he said quietly.

When we got to my apartment, we made love[55]. Then we lay together in my warm bed, and I fell asleep with my head on his shoulder.

At 7 a.m., I felt him kiss me softly. After that the door closed and Charlie was gone.

On Sunday, I visited the stores, cleaned my apartment, and wrote some notes. Then I spent a long time thinking.

The next morning, I went to see Lieutenant Dolan at the Santa Teresa police department. I gave him the letter that I'd found in Libby Glass's things. He took it carefully out of the envelope, holding one corner. He read it once, then he put it back in the envelope.

"Where did you get that?" he asked.

I told him. "Will you check it for fingerprints?"

"Let's talk about Sharon Napier first," he said.

"She's dead—I know that," I said carefully. We looked at each other in silence for a few moments. I decided to lie to him. "I know that, because a friend of mine in Las Vegas told me about it on the phone," I went on.

"Don't lie to me, Kinsey," he said. "You went to Las Vegas yourself. You've been investigating this case for two weeks and suddenly somebody gets killed."

"I had nothing to do with Sharon Napier's death, Lieutenant," I said. "I *didn't* go to Las Vegas. I went to Salton Sea. I went to find Greg Fife. If you don't believe me, call him. I was going to drive to Las Vegas after I talked to Greg."

"Who knew that you wanted to talk to Sharon Napier?"

"I don't think that Sharon was killed because she was going to talk to me." I said. "I heard that she was cheating some people at a casino in Las Vegas. She had enemies there. And don't ask me who they were, because I don't know."

The lieutenant sat and stared at me, then he said, "What have you found out about Libby Glass?"

"Not much. There's that letter. Nikki thinks that it's Laurence's writing, but there's something about it that I don't believe. Will you check it for fingerprints, please?"

"I'll think about it," Dolan said. "Now get out of here."

I went.

11

A Question for Colin

When I got to my office, two messages had been left with my answering service. The first one was from Garry Steinberg. I phoned him back immediately.

"Hi, Garry. How are you?"

"OK," he said. "I've got a little piece of information for you. I looked at Lyle Abernathy's job application this morning. Did you know that he used to work for a locksmith[56]?"

"No I didn't know that," I said.

"The locksmith was an old man called Fears. I phoned him when Lyle wanted a job here. Fears told me that Abernathy only worked for him for eight months. Fears suspected that the boy was stealing money from houses where he was fitting locks."

"That's great news, Garry!" I said. "It means that Lyle could have got into the Fifes' house easily, after their guard dog was killed. He could have got into Libby's apartment too. He could have poisoned both Laurence and Libby."

I thanked Garry and hung up.

The second message was from Gwen at K9 Korners. I called her.

"Hi, Gwen. It's Kinsey."

"Can you meet me for lunch?" she asked.

I thought for a moment. "Yes," I answered.

"Good. I'll meet you at the Palm Garden Restaurant in fifteen minutes."

———

I was drinking a glass of white wine when Gwen arrived. She sat down at my table and ordered some more wine from a waitress.

"I called your office on Tuesday," she said. "Your answering service said that you were in Los Angeles. I tried to call you there, but a strange woman answered the phone."

"That was Arlette," I said.

"She didn't seem to understand me, so I hung up."

The waitress brought Gwen's wine, and we both ordered salads. After the waitress went away, Gwen said, "I've decided to tell you about my lover."

"Oh?" I said. "Are you sure about that?"

"Yes," she replied. "I don't want you to spend a lot of time trying to find out his name. He died a few months ago. He'd been ill for a long time—he had a weak heart. His name was David Ray. He was Greg's schoolteacher, for a year.

David and his wife moved to San Francisco some time ago."

"And now he's dead," I said.

"Yes," she replied, "he's dead. If he wasn't, I wouldn't be telling you about him."

I thought that this was probably true. But I guessed that there was something that Gwen wasn't telling me—something that she *wanted* to tell me.

The waitress arrived with our salads and we ate in silence for several minutes.

"How are you getting on with your investigation?" Gwen asked at last. "Do you really expect to learn anything new after eight years have passed?"

I smiled. "It's possible that I will. People become careless when they're feeling safe."

Gwen and I talked for a while about my visits to Greg and Diane, but I was careful about what I told her. At 2:50 p.m., she looked at her watch.

"I've got to get back to work," she said.

"Gwen, when did you last see Colin?" I asked.

She looked at me quickly. "Colin?"

"Yes. I met him on Saturday," I said. "He's a fine boy."

"I don't know when I last saw him," Gwen said. Her face went red. Suddenly, she reminded me of someone—her daughter. Diane's face had gone red like this, just before she'd told me the truth about Bruno's death.

"When did I last see Colin?" she repeated. "It was at Diane's graduation[57] from junior high school."

I didn't believe her. I watched Gwen leave. I thought, "She could have told me about David Ray over the phone. She met me here because she wanted to tell me something else—something important. But then she couldn't say it."

But I'd had an idea. I'd need to talk to Nikki again, and maybe Colin.

After I left the restaurant, I went to Charlie's office.

"Can we have dinner together this evening?" I asked him.

"Yes," he said, smiling. "I'd like that. Come back here at six-fifteen."

Before I left, he held me in his arms and kissed me gently.

———

I drove to Nikki's beach house. She opened the door. There was paint on her hands.

"Oh, hi, Kinsey," she said. "Come in."

We went to the kitchen at the back of the house. Colin was sitting beside a cupboard which they had both been painting. He looked up at me and smiled.

"I want to ask Colin something," I said to Nikki. "But I have a question for you first. Did you leave town without Laurence during the months before he died? Were you away from Santa Teresa for more than a day or two?"

"Yes, I was away for a week," she said. "My father was ill and I went to Connecticut to visit him. Why do you ask?"

"Well, I've been thinking about why Colin believes that Gwen is 'Daddy's mother'. I'm worried about that, Nikki. Could Colin have seen Gwen during that time when you were away? He's a clever boy. He wouldn't think that Gwen was his grandmother—unless somebody told him that."

Nikki shook her head, but she didn't really answer my question. "Colin was only three and a half years old at that time, Kinsey," she said.

"Yes, I know that. But an hour ago, I asked Gwen when Colin last saw her. She said that it was at Diane's junior high school graduation."

74

"That's probably true," Nikki said.

"No, I don't think that it can be, Nikki," I replied. "Colin was about fourteen months old at the time of that graduation. If he last saw Gwen then, he wouldn't remember her at all. I think that Gwen lied to me. But why?"

"Maybe he did see her later and she just forgot about it," Nikki said. But she stared at me.

"Is it OK if we ask Colin about this?"

"Yes," she said.

I went into the living room. The photo album was on a small table. I turned the pages until I found the picture of Gwen. I took it out of the album and went back to the kitchen. I held the photo in front of Colin.

"Ask him if he can remember when he last saw this lady," I said to Nikki. "Ask him if she was here, at this house."

"Gwen?" Nikki said to me. "Why would Gwen have been here?"

"I don't know, Nikki. Just ask him, please."

Nikki touched the boy's shoulder. He looked at her, then at the photograph.

For the next minute or two, Nikki and her son had a conversation with their fingers. Then Nikki said, "He doesn't want to talk about it, Kinsey."

I was beginning to feel excited. I was thinking about what Charlotte Mercer had told me. Laurence Fife often fell in love with the same woman twice!

"Maybe Colin saw Laurence and Gwen with their arms around each other," I said to Nikki. "Maybe he saw them kissing. I think that Laurence told him that Gwen was 'Daddy's mother'."

Nikki stared at me. Then she turned to Colin and she

spoke with her fingers again. Colin shook his head, but he seemed frightened. Nikki looked back at me.

"I've just remembered something," she said. "Laurence *was* here alone with Colin once. He brought Colin here for a weekend. It was when I was in Connecticut. Greg and Diane stayed at the Montebello house with Mrs Voss."

"And if Gwen was here too—" I began.

"Please stop this, Kinsey! I don't want to talk about this any more," Nikki said.

"Nikki, please ask Colin why he called Gwen 'Daddy's mother'."

Nikki looked very unhappy. But she asked the boy the question with her fingers. Colin answered, then he pointed to his head.

"Gwen *was* here," Nikki said to me quietly. "Colin says that she looked like a grandmother, because she had gray hair."

"Was Gwen's hair gray eight years ago?" I asked her.

"Oh, yes," Nikki said. "Gwen's hair went gray when she was in her thirties."

Colin was calm again now, but I could see anger in Nikki's eyes. "But Laurence hated Gwen," she said. She started to cry. "Why did he bring her here? Oh, I really don't want to know any more about this!"

"Listen, Nikki!" I said. "You paid me five thousand dollars to find out what happened to Laurence. If you don't like the truth, I can give you your money back. Do you want me to go on with this investigation?"

She thought for a moment. "Yes, I do," she said.

I left soon after that. Nikki was angry and unhappy. I had no reason to feel bad about doing my job. But I did feel bad!

———

Colin answered, then he pointed to his head.

I'd finished work for the day. I went to Charlie's office building. He was waiting for me at the top of the stairs.

"I want a drink," I said, "and I want some food. I hope that you're a good cook, Charlie, because I'm not."

"We can't go to my house, Kinsey," he said. "John Powers, my law partner, is out of town and I have to go and feed his dogs. I'll make us a meal at his house. It's at the beach."

"OK, that's great," I said.

Charlie locked the office door and I followed him out to the parking lot[58]. He walked to his pale-blue Mercedes, but I was already going towards my own car. It was parked in the street.

"Don't you want to ride with me?" he asked.

"I'll follow you," I replied. "I don't like being without my VW."

Charlie drove slowly to John Powers's house at the beach, and I followed him. Powers's house wasn't far from Nikki's beach house. It had a carport[59] with space for two cars. There was one car already in the carport—a Lincoln. I guessed that it was Powers's own car.

The dogs were the kind that I hate. They were guard dogs. They were big and noisy, and they jumped up at me. We took them onto the beach, where they ran around happily for half an hour. After that, we went back into the house. I followed Charlie to the kitchen, and he found a bottle of wine and two glasses.

"Do you often do this for Mr Powers?" I asked him.

"Powers has to be out of town for a few days of every month," he replied. "I always check the house and feed his dogs when he's away."

I drank some wine. "Charlie, did you know that Laurence

Fife once had an affair with Sharon Napier's mother?" I asked him. "It happened some time before Sharon went to work for him. She blackmailed him to give her the job. It was her revenge for what he did to her mother."

Charlie looked surprised. "Who told you that? I never knew about it, and I knew Laurence for many years."

"You didn't know about Mrs Napier, Charlie?" I said. "Are you sure? That's what you said about Libby Glass at first."

His smile disappeared. "Is that why you wanted to meet me this evening, Kinsey?" he said. "You wanted to ask me questions?"

"No, Charlie. I came out here to get away from work for a few hours."

"Then why are you asking me all these questions?" he said angrily. "I don't like them." He looked down at his glass, then spoke carefully. "I know that you have a job to do, and I'll help you when I can. But you're not a nice person when you start talking about your work."

Now I was angry too. "I'm sorry," I said coldly. "People give me information, but I need to check it."

"Well, I don't like all these questions," he said again.

"I've had a bad day, Charlie," I said. "I don't want to argue with you."

I put down my wine glass and walked out of the house.

12

Who Killed Laurence Fife?

I'd been at home for an hour before I stopped feeling angry. I poured a big glass of wine and sat down at my desk to work. Three hours later, I made a sandwich and I read through my notes.

Then there was a knock at my front door. I looked at my watch—12:25 a.m. I walked to the door but I didn't open it.

"Yes?" I said.

"It's me," Charlie Scorsoni said. "Can I come in?"

I opened the door. "I'm sorry, Kinsey," he said.

I let him in and closed the door behind him. He watched me put my notes away in my desk.

"Do you want a drink?" I asked.

He shook his head. "No. Listen, Kinsey, I'm sorry about getting angry."

I held out my hand.

"I'm sorry, too, Charlie," I said. He kissed my fingers, and put his arms around me. I knew then how much I wanted him. We moved towards the bed.

He was gone again by 2 a.m. He had to start work early the next day, and so did I.

———

I got to my office at nine o'clock the next morning. I checked with my answering service. Lieutenant Dolan had tried to phone me. I called the Santa Teresa Police Department and asked for him.

"We couldn't find any good fingerprints on that letter," he told me.

"What about the handwriting?" I asked. "Is it Laurence

Fife's handwriting?"

"Yes, we're sure of that," he replied.

I hung up. Then I went to the window and looked down at the street. I'd been sure that Laurence Fife hadn't written that letter. But I'd been wrong and I didn't like it.

I worked at the office for the rest of the morning, and the first half of the afternoon. I went home at three o'clock. When I got home, the letter was still worrying me. But suddenly I had an idea. I found Charlotte Mercer's phone number and I called her.

"I can't talk to you now," Charlotte told me angrily. "I don't want you to call me when my husband is at home."

"OK. But I have just one question," I said. "You told me about Sharon Napier's mother. Do you remember Mrs Napier's first name?"

"It was Elizabeth," she said quickly. "Now leave me alone!" And she slammed down the phone.

I put my own phone down and smiled. I had been right. That letter *wasn't* written to Libby Glass. Laurence Fife had written it to Elizabeth Napier, years before he knew Libby. But how did Libby get the letter? And who wanted it back now? Who was the person who'd been searching the boxes in the basement of the Glasses' apartment building? Who was the person who'd shot at the light so that I didn't see him— or her?

If my guess was right, Laurence and Libby had never had an affair. This meant that there must be some other reason why someone killed them. But what was it?

"Maybe Laurence Fife and Lyle Abernathy were working together, doing something illegal[60]," I thought. "Maybe Libby found out about this. Maybe Lyle killed them both to protect

81

himself. And maybe Sharon Napier knew about it, too. Maybe Lyle killed her before she could tell me about it."

But then I remembered that a key to Libby's apartment had been found in Laurence's office desk. Somebody had wanted the police to think that Libby was having an affair with Laurence Fife. But could Lyle have put the key there? I didn't think so!

I thought again about Sharon Napier's death. When the police had investigated the deaths of Laurence and Libby, alibis[61] hadn't been important. Nobody knew exactly when the oleander had been put into the capsules, so the suspects hadn't needed alibis. But I knew exactly when Sharon Napier had been shot. For that murder, an alibi was going to be very important!

I took my notes from my desk and I looked at the first piece of paper in my file. On it was a list of all the people that I'd talked to about the case. Two of the names were of people from Santa Teresa who knew about my trip to Las Vegas. They both knew that I was going to talk to Sharon. Did either of them have an alibi for the time when she was killed? I needed to find out about that. One of the names was Nikki Fife. The other was Charlie Scorsoni!

I wanted to take Charlie off my list, but where had he been on the night that Sharon died? I knew that he'd been in Denver earlier in that week, because I'd called him there myself. Arlette said that he'd also phoned from Tucson and again from Santa Teresa. But she couldn't prove that he'd been in those places when he called. He could have called from anywhere—from Las Vegas, for example! So perhaps Charlie didn't have an alibi for the time of Sharon's death.

I wanted to believe that Charlie was innocent. I liked

him very much, and I'd made love with him. For half an hour, I tried to think about something else. But I couldn't. I phoned Charlie at his home.

"Hi, it's Kinsey," I said when he answered.

"Kinsey, hello," he said softly. "I was hoping that you'd call me. Can I meet you?"

"No, listen, Charlie," I said. "I don't want us to meet until I've finished this investigation."

There was a long silence. "OK," he said at last.

"I'm sorry, Charlie," I said.

"Do whatever you want," he said coldly. He hung up.

I felt bad. I wanted to call him back right away. But I had to go on with the investigation, and there was something that I needed to do immediately. I picked up the phone again and I called Gwen.

"This is Kinsey," I said. "I think that we should talk again. Do you know Rosie's Bar, near the beach?"

"Yes, I know the place, Kinsey," she said.

"Can you meet me there in half an hour? It's important."

"OK. I'll be there as soon as I can."

———

Rosie's Bar was nearly empty. I bought a glass of wine and I sat at a table near the window. Gwen arrived forty-five minutes later. She smiled when she said hello, but I could see that she was worried. Had she guessed what I was going to say to her?

She ordered a whisky, then she looked at me and waited for me to speak.

"I talked to Colin," I said. "He remembered you."

"Well, that's nice," she replied. "I haven't seen him for years, of course. I told you that."

Her drink arrived and I paid for it. She waited for me to speak again.

"You didn't tell me that you'd had an affair with Laurence after your divorce," I said.

She tried to laugh. "Who, *me*? With *him*? Are you *serious*, Kinsey?"

"Colin saw you at the beach house. It was that weekend when Nikki was in Connecticut."

I watched her face. "OK," she said at last. "I made love with Laurence there once. I met him at the Palm Garden Restaurant one day, and he told me that Nikki was out of town. I was surprised that he spoke to me. But I was lonely and he was kind to me. So I went to the beach house with him."

She drank a lot of the whisky.

"You made love with him more than once after your divorce, Gwen," I said. "I think that you had an affair with him. He'd been meeting Charlotte Mercer again, but he broke up with her and started an affair with someone else. Charlotte told me that his new affair was very secret, very exciting! I think that you were his new lover."

"Oh, why does it matter?" she said. "He'd been having affairs for years."

I didn't answer for a minute. I was thinking. I'd been right so far. Now I had another idea!

"Gwen, I think that *you* killed Laurence," I said.

Gwen's face went pale. She started to say something but couldn't speak.

"Do you want to tell me about it?" I asked her softly.

She shook her head and looked away from me. She was trying not to cry.

"I think that you killed Laurence."

"You waited until Laurence and Nikki and Greg went to Salton Sea for the weekend. Then you used Diane's keys to get into the Montebello house. You put powdered oleander into some of Laurence's allergy capsules. You were careful not to leave any fingerprints. Then you left."

"I put the oleander in *one* capsule," she said at last. She spoke quickly now. "I hated him! He took everything from me. He took my kids, he took my money, he—"

She put her hands over her eyes for a moment. Then she finished the whisky.

"Then why did you have an affair with him?" I asked.

"I don't know," she said. "Perhaps that was part of my revenge. I knew that I could make him come back to me. I'd had an affair with somebody else while I was married to Laurence and he'd hated that. He had to prove that he was better than my lover. Oh, God, Laurence was a terrible man! I wish that I could kill him again!"

"But what about Nikki?" I said. I was angry now. "She spent eight years in jail for something that she didn't do!"

"I didn't think that Nikki would go to jail," Gwen said quietly. "But I certainly didn't want to go to jail myself."

"Did you kill the dog, too?"

"No. The dog *was* hit by a car. On that Sunday morning, I drove Diane over to the house when she remembered about Bruno. She found his body. She was ill that weekend, and she was very upset about the dog. She went to bed as soon as we got back to my house. While she was asleep, I took her keys and I went to Montebello again. That's when I put the oleander in the capsule."

"It was more than one capsule, Gwen," I said. "What about Libby Glass? You poisoned her too! And last week you shot Sharon Napier!"

Gwen seemed surprised. "I don't know what you're talking about," she said after a moment.

"Don't lie to me, Gwen!" I said, standing up. "I don't believe that!"

She didn't understand my anger. "What are you going to do?" she asked.

"I'm going to give all this information to Nikki," I said. "She paid for the investigation. She can decide what to do next."

I walked away from the table, towards the door. Gwen ran after me and pulled my shoulder, but I pushed her away.

"Find yourself a good attorney, Gwen," I said. "You're going to need one."

13

The Letter

I went home, locked the door of my apartment, and called Nikki. There was no reply.

I'd been paid to find out who killed Laurence Fife and I now I *had* found out. But I'd been thinking carefully as I drove home. There were things which I still didn't understand—things that still didn't make sense. Now I didn't really believe that Gwen had killed Libby Glass eight years ago. I was starting to believe that she *had* only put oleander in one capsule. And I certainly didn't believe that Gwen had driven to Las Vegas and shot Sharon Napier.

So there was a *second* murderer! I'd wanted to believe that the same person had killed all three people, but I'd been wrong. Gwen had killed Laurence Fife by poisoning him with oleander. Then a few days later, someone else had used the same poison to kill Libby Glass. Why? So that the police would believe that the two people were killed by the same murderer! And they *had* believed that. They'd believed that Nikki had killed both Laurence and Libby. But Nikki *hadn't* killed Laurence. And if she hadn't killed him, why would she have killed Libby? And why would she have killed Sharon? Nikki was innocent, I was sure about that now. So who had killed them? Lyle? Charlie?

I thought about Lyle Abernathy. He'd known about Laurence's death before Libby died. Libby had told him about it herself. He knew about the oleander in Laurence's capsule. He could have copied the idea and killed Libby! But could he have put the key in Laurence Fife's desk? I had to ask some more questions.

I called my answering service. "I'm going to Los Angeles again," I said. "If Nikki Fife phones, give her the number of the Hacienda Motor Lodge. Tell her to call me there as soon as possible. But I don't want anyone else to know where I am. That's important."

The drive to Los Angeles calmed me down. The night air was warm, and I got to the Hacienda at 11:05 p.m. I went straight to room number two and I got into bed.

———

In the morning, as I walked past the motel office, Arlette called to me. She was holding up the phone.

"Somebody wants to speak to you," she said.

I went in and took the phone from her.

"Hello?" I said.

"Kinsey, this is Nikki." She sounded frightened.

"Is there something wrong?"

"Gwen's dead," she said.

"But I talked to her last night!"

"She was killed this morning," Nikki went on. "A car hit her. The driver didn't stop."

Was I surprised? No, not really.

"Listen Nikki, I've got to check some things here," I said quickly. "Call Lieutenant Dolan and find out exactly what happened to Gwen. Her death probably wasn't an accident. I'll phone you as soon as I get back to Santa Teresa."

I went back to my room to think. Could Gwen's death have been an accident? I didn't think so.

———

I drove to the house in Sherman Oaks where Lyle Abernathy had been working. His truck was parked outside it. I got my gun from my briefcase, then I locked my car and went around the side of the house. I found Lyle near the rear door. He turned to look at me.

I held the gun in front of me. "I want some answers and I want them now," I said. "I don't want to shoot you, Lyle, but I will if you don't tell me the truth!"

He looked at the gun.

"You told me that you last saw Libby on the Wednesday before her death," I said. "But I don't believe that, Lyle. When did you really last see her?"

"I didn't kill her," he said.

"Tell me when you last saw her!" I shouted.

"OK. I saw her on the Saturday," he said.

"The day that she died, is that right?"

"I didn't kill her," he said.

"That's right, but I didn't kill her. We had a big argument. She was very upset when I left."

"OK, what else happened?"

He was silent. Then he put his hands over his face and I heard him crying.

"Tell me, Lyle," I said, more gently.

"I gave her a tranquilizer[62]," he said. "She asked me to get her one. I found a bottle of them in her bathroom. I gave her a capsule from it. Oh, God! I loved her so much."

"Go on, Lyle," I said.

"I left her after that, but later I felt terrible, and I went back. The apartment door wasn't locked. I found Libby on the bathroom floor. She was dead. I was afraid that the police would find my fingerprints on the tranquilizer bottle. I was afraid that they'd think that I'd killed her. So I cleaned the apartment. I didn't tell anybody that Libby was dead."

"And you took the tranquilizers with you when you left?"

He nodded. "Yes. I took the bottle." He looked at me. "I didn't poison Libby. You've got to believe me!"

I did believe him.

"And you didn't break open the boxes in the Glasses' basement, last week," I said.

He shook his head. I put the gun in my pocket.

"Are you going to tell the police about me?" he asked.

"No," I said.

I went back to the car. I had one more place to visit, then I could drive back to Santa Teresa. I knew now who the second killer was.

———

I went to the offices of Haycraft and McNiece. Garry Steinberg was in his room. He looked happy to see me.

"You look very tired," he said.

"Yes. But I'm sure that I know the truth about my case now," I said. "Can we talk for a few minutes?"

"Yes," he said. "Do you want some coffee?"

I sat down. "No, thanks. I need to check something with you. You told me that Libby was putting the Fife and Scorsoni firm's accounts onto your company's computer."

"That's right," he said.

"If one of the attorneys had been stealing money from the firm's clients, could Libby have discovered that quickly?"

"Yes," Garry replied. "Do you think that Fife was stealing money from his clients?"

"No, Garry," I said. "But I do think that Charlie Scorsoni was stealing money.

"People have said that Libby was having an affair with a Santa Teresa attorney. Everybody thought that the attorney was Fife, because he and Libby both died of oleander poisoning, and there was a key to Libby's apartment in Fife's desk. And everybody thought that one person killed both Fife *and* Libby. But that was wrong. I know who killed Fife. It was his first wife, Gwen. She's told me about it. But Gwen didn't kill Libby.

"I think that Charlie Scorsoni had started an affair with Libby a month or two before she died. He knew that she would find problems in the firm's accounts. But he thought that, if she loved him, she wouldn't tell anybody about the problems. But I think that when Libby did find the problems, she refused to tell lies for him. So Scorsoni killed her before she could make trouble for him. I think that he put that key in Fife's desk, so that the police would think that Laurence had been her lover. I can't prove *any* of this, of course."

"Maybe I can prove that Scorsoni was stealing money," Garry said. "I've got the Fife and Scorsoni accounts on my desk now. I'll start looking at them this afternoon."

I drove back to Santa Teresa, thinking about Charlie Scorsoni. I was angry! Charlie had had an affair with Libby to protect himself from trouble, I was sure of that. And he'd done the same thing with me. Now I had to know where he was when Sharon Napier was killed. Did he have an alibi? I'd have to find out. He could have flown from Denver to Las Vegas. He could have got the address of my motel from my answering service. Then he could have followed me to Sharon's apartment and to the Fremont Casino.

I suddenly remembered what had happened in the coffee shop there. Sharon had seen someone that she knew behind me. Maybe that was Charlie! Sharon must have known that Charlie, and not Laurence Fife, had had an affair with Libby Glass. Maybe she'd been blackmailing Charlie for years. It was possible.

But why hadn't he killed her before? Why had he needed to follow me? Was it possible that Charlie hadn't known where Sharon was until I found her? Yes, he'd told me that himself! He'd said that she owed him some money. He'd asked me to tell him where she was living, when I found her!

And something else was possible too. Maybe Charlie had now guessed that Nikki hadn't killed Laurence. Maybe he'd guessed that Gwen had killed him. Maybe he'd guessed that I would make Gwen tell the truth. If that happened, he knew that the police would start looking again for Libby's killer. He would be in danger. Had he killed Gwen to stop her talking to me? Yes, that was possible. Charlie hadn't known that

Gwen had already told me the truth, because I'd stopped talking to him before I knew about Gwen's guilt.

If Charlie had killed Gwen with his car, the police would be able to prove it. Gwen's hair or blood would be on the Mercedes. And paint from the car would be on Gwen's clothes.

I was sad and angry when I drove back to Santa Teresa. I tried not to think about Charlie and me.

———

I drove straight to my office. The bills that I had taken from Sharon's apartment were still in my car. I picked them up and took them inside with me. Maybe there would be some useful information in them. I sat at my desk and looked through them quickly. One of them was Sharon's phone bill for the month of March, and it was very interesting. Sharon had called numbers in Santa Teresa three times during the month. Two of the calls were to Charlie Scorsoni's office. I didn't recognize the number of the third call, but I had an idea about it. I picked up my Santa Teresa phone book and I found the number for John Powers's beach house. I was right! Sharon's third call had been to that number.

Next, I phoned Ruth at Charlie's office.

"Hi, Ruth. This is Kinsey Millhone. Is Charlie there?"

"Hi, Kinsey," Ruth said. "No, he's not here. He's in Santa Maria for the next two days."

"Maybe you can help me, Ruth," I said. "Do you remember someone named Sharon Napier phoning Charlie—about six or eight weeks ago?"

"The woman who used to work for him?" Ruth replied. "Yes, she phoned him several times."

"Did she call on Friday, March twenty-first? Do you

remember?" I said.

"Oh, yes," Ruth said. "Charlie was at Mr Powers's house when Sharon Napier called. She said that she had to talk to him. She said that it was very important. I called him there and he told me to give her Mr Powers's number. So I did."

"Thanks, Ruth," I said. "Now the other thing I need to ask you about is Charlie's visit to Tucson."

"Tucson?" she said suspiciously. Her voice told me that she was beginning to ask herself why I wanted to know these things. "Well—"

"It doesn't matter, Ruth," I said quickly. "I can phone Charlie about this when he gets back."

"Well, I can give you the number of his motel in Santa Maria," she said. "You could call him there."

"Thanks, Ruth," I said. I wrote down the number. But I knew that I would never call it.

My next call was to Lieutenant Dolan. He wasn't in his office. I left a message asking him to phone me when he got back.

Then I phoned Nikki at her beach house.

"Hi, Nikki," I said. "It's Kinsey. Did you get any more information from Dolan about Gwen's death?"

"He didn't want to tell me anything," she replied. "But he did tell me that the car that killed her was black."

"Black?" I said. "Are you sure?" Had I been wrong again? Charlie's Mercedes was pale blue.

"That's what Dolan told me."

"OK," I said. "Do you remember the letter that I showed you—the letter that Laurence wrote? Well, I think that it was written to a woman named Elizabeth Napier, not to Libby Glass. I think that Mrs Napier was the first woman that

95

Laurence had an affair with after he married Gwen. Elizabeth was Sharon Napier's mother."

"I did hear something about that affair," Nikki said. "I never knew the woman's name—Laurence never talked about her. But I heard that her husband divorced her."

"But why did Libby Glass have that letter, Nikki?" I asked. "Did Laurence get it back from Elizabeth Napier? If he did, why did he give it to Libby?"

"I think that Charlie Scorsoni had the letter at one time, Kinsey," Nikki replied. "Before Charlie worked with Laurence, he was with the firm who worked for the husband in that divorce case. Charlie did steal a letter to help Laurence. Charlotte Mercer told me that. Laurence didn't want the letter to be read at the divorce hearing. He was a married man, and he didn't want people to know that he had a lover. So he spoke to Charlie, who had been his friend for years. And the next day, the letter wasn't in the law firm's file. And soon after that, Charlie started working for Laurence's firm."

I hung up. So it was Charlie who broke open the boxes in Mrs Glass's basement, not Lyle! But he hadn't taken anything away from the basement—he'd left something there! He'd put the letter in Libby's things. He wanted me to find it. He'd hoped that it would make me believe his story about an affair between Libby and Laurence.

At last everything made sense. Gwen had killed Laurence Fife. But Charlie Scorsoni had killed Libby Glass, and he'd put her apartment key in Fife's desk. Eight years later, he'd killed Sharon Napier. Sharon had known about his affair with Libby and was blackmailing him about it. And now he'd killed Gwen.

14

The End of the Affair

I wrote a report for Nikki, explaining everything that I'd discovered. Then I looked up Charlie's address in the phone book and I drove there.

There was no car outside the house. I walked up to the garage at the side of the house and I looked through the window. Charlie's Mercedes wasn't inside.

It was getting dark now. I looked at my watch—6:45 p.m. I decided to drive to Nikki's beach house. I could give her my report right away.

To get to Nikki's house, I had to drive past John Powers's house. As I passed it, I had an idea. I stopped my car. I put my gun in my pocket and picked up my flashlight. I got out of the car and locked it.

The street was quiet—no cars, no people. Powers's house was in darkness. Was he still out of town? And where were his guard dogs?

I turned on the flashlight and I walked carefully to the carport. John Powers's car was inside—his Lincoln. I'd seen it there before, but I'd forgotten its color. It was black! I shone my flashlight onto the front of the car. The right headlight was broken. The right-hand side of the fender[63] was broken too. I tried not to think about it hitting Gwen's body.

Then I heard a car stop suddenly in the street near the house. After a moment, I heard it start again and I saw headlights coming towards the carport. I pulled my gun out of my pocket and turned off the flashlight. Charlie's pale-blue Mercedes was coming towards me. He'd phoned Ruth and she'd told him about my call. He'd come back to Santa Teresa

97

at once. He *knew* that I'd found out the truth!

I turned and ran. I ran through the back yard, towards the sea. There were narrow wooden steps leading down to the beach. I started to run down the steps. Suddenly, I heard the two dogs running behind me. I turned and saw one of them on the steps, just above my head. I stopped, put my hand around one of its front legs, and pulled hard. I threw the dog down onto the beach. The other dog was moving more slowly and carefully towards the top of the steps.

I turned again and I fell down the last few steps onto the sand. When I got up, the first dog was running towards me. I waited until it was close to me, then I slammed the gun down onto its head. The dog barked loudly, but it stood still.

I moved quickly towards the sea, watching the dog all the time. In half a minute, my feet were in the water. I started walking in the sea, a few yards from the shore, holding my gun in front of me. Then I looked up, and I saw Charlie at the top of the wooden steps. He had switched on all the lights in the house. He was staring down at me.

There were big rocks at the end of the beach, and I quickly climbed over them. I couldn't see Powers's house now, and the dogs hadn't followed me. But was Charlie following me? I couldn't be sure. Maybe he'd gone back to his car. Maybe he was driving along the street next to the shore. If he was, we'd both arrive at Ludlow Beach at the same time. But Ludlow Beach was a busy place. There would certainly be other people there, and cars in the streets. "Charlie couldn't hurt me there, could he?" I thought.

I began to run.

After some minutes, I saw Ludlow Beach ahead of me. There were lots of lights there. I stopped running and I

Then I looked up, and I saw Charlie at the top of the wooden steps.

walked slowly out of the water, onto the sand. Beyond the sand, there was a flat parking lot. And beyond the parking lot was the main street. I had to get to the street!

A moment later, I knew that I had a problem. Charlie's Mercedes was already in the parking lot! The headlights were switched on, shining onto the beach. There were no other people or cars in the parking lot. And there was no way that I could get to the street without Charlie seeing me.

But where was Charlie? Was he sitting in the car, waiting for me? Or was he waiting among the palm trees which grew at the edges of the parking lot?

I walked back into the sea again and I went out further from the shore. The water was very cold, but it would be difficult for Charlie to see me in the dark sea. I held my gun up high out of the water as I moved. I watched the beach and I looked for Charlie. His car headlights were still on. Soon, I'd moved on two hundred yards past the parking lot. Where was Charlie now?

I came out of the water again and up the beach. I moved carefully to my right across the sand. And suddenly I saw Charlie! He wasn't far away, but he hadn't seen me. He was twenty yards to my left. I got down onto the sand and I started to pull myself along with my arms. After a minute or two, I was among the palm trees. It was dark there.

I looked to my left and I saw Charlie again. Then he disappeared, and a few moments later I heard his car start. Was he leaving the parking lot? Was he going to drive farther along the beach?

There was a big trash bin[64] at the edge of the parking lot. As Charlie started to turn his car, I ran over to it. I lifted the metal lid, and I climbed inside. The smell was terrible as I pushed myself down between pieces of old food and empty cola cans. I held the metal lid open above my head and looked out. Now Charlie's car had turned again and it was moving towards the trash bin. In a second, the headlights of the Mercedes would shine onto my hiding place. I closed the lid quickly.

I heard Charlie get out of the car. I heard him walking towards the bin.

"Kinsey, I know you're here," he said.

I tried not to move. I tried not to breathe.

"Kinsey, what's wrong? Don't be afraid of me. I won't hurt you—don't you know that, Kinsey? I've never hurt anyone."

His voice was soft and kind. Was I wrong about him? Had I made a terrible mistake?

After a moment, I heard him moving away. Carefully, I lifted the lid a couple of inches and looked out. Charlie was looking at the sea. He turned back and I quickly closed the lid again. But the metal lid made a noise and Charlie heard it! I could hear him coming closer. I held the gun up. My hand was shaking. Maybe I was crazy. Maybe I was wrong about everything. In one second, I would know!

Charlie lifted the lid of the trash bin and looked down at me. In his hand was a long knife. He was going to kill me.

I shot him.

———

I still think about Charlie. I never wanted to kill anyone. I had to do it. But maybe Gwen would have said that. And maybe Charlie would have said that too.

Points for Understanding

1

1 Who is Nikki Fife and how old is she at the beginning of this story?
2 "You told Nikki to come and see me," Kinsey says to Lieutenant Dolan. "So maybe you aren't sure about Nikki's guilt—you have doubts. Is this right?" "My doubts have nothing to do with Laurence Fife's death," Dolan replies.
(a) Dolan's doubts have to do with something other than Laurence Fife's death. What?
(b) What is his real reason for sending Nikki to Kinsey?

2

1 How long have Charlie Scorsoni and John Powers been law partners?
2 Kinsey asks Gwen which people were happy about Laurence's death. "If you have an hour, I'll give you a list," Gwen tells her. What does Gwen mean?

3

1 Nikki and Kinsey visit the Montebello house. "Who had keys to this house at the time of your husband's death?" Kinsey asks her. Why do you think that Kinsey asks this question?
2 "Laurence discovered that Gwen was having an affair herself. He had his affair with me to prove that he didn't care about *her* affair," Nikki tells Kinsey.
Did Nikki believe that Laurence didn't care about Gwen's affair? Give a reason for your answer.

4

Gwen tells Kinsey to talk to Charlotte Mercer about Laurence's affair with her. Then Gwen laughs, and says, "If she wants to know who sent you, then please tell her!"
Why do you think that Gwen says this?

5

Why does Grace Glass put headphones over her husband's ears when Kinsey starts asking questions about Libby?

6

In this chapter, Kinsey asks Lyle Abernathy some questions. His answer to one of the questions could help Kinsey's investigation into Libby's death. But Kinsey doesn't understand the importance of Lyle's answer. Which of Lyle's answers do you think that this is?

7

1 "This girl is not trying to be helpful," Kinsey thinks when she talks to the receptionist at Haycraft and McNiece. Why does she think this?
2 Why does Kinsey take the cigarette packet from Sharon Napier's pocket?

8

1 Kinsey asks Greg Fife about the family's trip to Salton Sea which happened just before Laurence's death. "I was seventeen then. God, I was stupid!" Greg says.
   (a) Why does he say this?
   (b) Which other sentences in this chapter help to explain his words?
2 In Chapter 1, Nikki told Kinsey that Greg and Diane Fife blame her for their father's death. But does Diane really think that Nikki killed Laurence? What does she say in *this* chapter which makes you doubt it?

9

In this chapter, Kinsey starts to think that Nikki might be a murderer. Explain why she thinks this.

10

Kinsey gives Lieutenant Dolan the letter which she had found in Libby's things. She wants him to check it for fingerprints. Why?

11

1 Gwen tells Kinsey that Colin last saw her at Diane's junior high school graduation. Kinsey doesn't believe her. Why not?
2 Kinsey remembers something that Charlotte Mercer has told her. She asks Colin a question.
   (a) What does she remember Charlotte saying?
   (b) How might Colin's answer help Kinsey's investigation?

12

1 Kinsey asks herself if it is possible that Lyle Abernathy killed both Laurence and Libby. She decides that Lyle was probably not the killer. Why does she think this?
2 Kinsey tells Charlie Scorsoni that she does not want to meet him again until she has finished her investigation. Why do you think that she tells him this?

13

1 Lyle tells Kinsey what really happened on the day of Libby's death. Why is this information important to her?
2 Kinsey talks to Ruth, Charlie's secretary.
   (a) What information does Kinsey get from her?
   (b) Why is this information important to Kinsey?

14

Kinsey looks at John Powers's black Lincoln car. One headlight and part of the fender were broken. What does this tell Kinsey about the death of Gwen Fife?

Glossary

Note
This book is written in American English. Here are the British words for some American vocabulary that you will find in this story.

AMERICAN ENGLISH	BRITISH ENGLISH
apartment	flat
attorney	lawyer
bathrobe	dressing gown
center	centre
check	cheque
coffee shop	café
fender	bumper
flashlight	torch
guy	man
highway	motorway
jail (*n,v*)	prison (*n,v*)
mom (mother)	mum (mother)
parking lot	car park
yard	garden

1 ***private detective*** (page 4)
   Kinsey does not work for the police. She is a *private detective* or *private investigator*. People pay her to find things or people, or to find out the truth. Each of her jobs is called a *case*. Sometimes she has to *investigate someone's death*. After she has *finished her investigation*, she has to *write a report*.

2 ***statement*** (page 6)
   Kinsey has told the police what has happened. She has written down her words and then signed her name. This is a *signed statement*.

3 ***client*** (page 6)
   someone who pays Kinsey to do some work for them, is her *client*.

4 ***answering service*** (page 6)
   Kinsey doesn't have a secretary who works in her office. When she leaves town, she needs someone to answer her phone and to give messages to her clients (see above). Kinsey uses an *answering service*. Her phone calls go to the answering service's office. The people in the answering service then take messages from anyone who calls Kinsey's phone number.

5 *divorce attorney* (page 6)

an *attorney* is a lawyer. A *divorce attorney* is a lawyer who works for people who do not want to be married anymore. When two people want to get divorced, a lawyer helps them to decide who owns their property and their money. Attorneys work together in a *law firm*. Attorneys who have worked together for a long time in their firm are often *partners*. They own the firm.

6 *guilty* (page 7)

if someone breaks the law they are *guilty* of a crime. If someone is accused of a crime which they did not do, they are *innocent*. If there is a trial in a law court, the court decides about a person's *guilt* or *innocence*.

7 *affair* (page 7)

to have an *affair* with someone who is not your wife or husband is to have a sexual relationship with that person.

8 *done my time* (page 9)

at her trial, Nikki was found guilty (see above) of murder and she was sent to jail for eight years. *I've done my time* is an informal way of saying "I spent time in jail".

9 *allergies* (page 9)

when you become ill because of animal hair, or dust, or plants, you have an *allergy* to these things—you are *allergic* to them. You can also be allergic to some kinds of food or drink. People who have allergies often cannot breathe easily and they sneeze and cough.

10 *capsule* (page 9)

very small soft gelatin containers which are filled with medicine. When you swallow the *capsules,* the gelatin breaks up inside your stomach so that the medicine comes out.

11 *powdered oleander* (page 9)

oleander is a plant with dark green leaves and bright red or white flowers. It grows in warm, dry countries. *Powdered* means that the leaves have been dried and then crushed until they are a soft, fine dust.

12 *fingerprints* (page 10)

marks made by your fingers when you touch something. Everybody has lines on the skin at end of their fingers. Everybody's *fingerprints* are different. Police study the fingerprints so that they can find out who has done a crime.

13 *divorce hearing* (page 10)

when two people want to end their marriage, they go to see a judge at a *divorce hearing*. Both the man and the woman have attorneys who explain to the judge about their marriage. The judge then decides how the couple's property and money will be divided between them and who will look after their children.

14 *accountant* (page 11)
someone who checks what you have earned and what you have spent so that you pay the correct tax to the government. This person is working on your *personal accounts*. Accountants also prepare documents for business and companies.

15 *blame* (page 14)
Kinsey is asking if Laurence's older children thought that Nikki had killed their father.

16 *power over* (page 14)
if you have *power over someone*, you can make that person do things that they don't want to do.

17 *K9 Korners* (page 16)
if you say "K9", it sounds like the word "canine". This is a joke. "Canine" means anything about dogs. Gwen has used "K" instead of "C" for the spelling of "corners" so that there is a "k" sound in both words.

18 *left all his money to*—*to leave something to someone* (page 20)
if you *leave* money or property to someone, that person has the money or property after your death.

19 *deaf* (page 20)
a *deaf* person is unable to hear.

20 *phone booth* (page 21)
a tall box that people go into to make phone calls. *Phone booths* are found on streets, in stores, hotels and restaurants and in railroad stations and airports.

21 *housekeeper* (page 21)
someone who works in a house. A *housekeeper* takes care of all the people who live in the house, and also makes sure that the house is clean and tidy.

22 *air pollution* (page 22)
air which is difficult to breathe because it has smoke or dangerous chemicals in it is *polluted*. *Air pollution* in cities is often caused by the smoke from cars, trucks and buses.

23 *guard dog* (page 22)
a large dog that is used to look after people, houses or property.

24 *suspected*—*to suspect* (page 24)
if you *suspect* someone of doing something, you think that they did it. Someone who is *suspected* of doing something is a *suspect*. The verb is pronounced sus**pect**, the noun is pronounced **sus**pect.

25 **calm down** (page 27)
become quiet after being angry or upset.

26 **broke up with**—*to break up with someone* (page 28)
end an affair or sexual relationship with someone.

27 **phone book** (page 28)
a book which gives *lists* of all the phone numbers, as well as the names and addresses, of people and companies who have phones in a town or a city. Most towns and cities in the world have phone books. If someone is *listed* in the phone book, then you will be able to find their phone number and address written in it.

28 **had been at work on her** (page 29)
Charlotte Mercer has been to a hospital and had operations on her face and body. A surgeon had cut, pulled and sewn her skin to make her look younger.

29 **blackmail** (page 32)
when someone *blackmails* you they know a secret about you and ask you for money. If you will not pay them the money, they will tell everyone your secret.

30 **revenge** (page 32)
if someone hurts you or does something bad to you, and then you hurt them, this is your *revenge*.

31 **motel** (page 33)
a hotel close to a highway. At a motel, you can park your car near your hotel room. The word is made from "motor" and "hotel".

32 **wheelchair** (page 34)
a chair on wheels. *Wheelchairs* are used by people who are ill, or who cannot walk.

33 **headphones** (page 34)
things that fit over your ears so that you can listen to a TV, a radio, or to an audio system. You can hear the sounds from the *headphones*, but other people can't.

34 **changed his mind** (page 35)
Lyle was going to study to be a lawyer. But then he decided that he didn't want to do this—he *changed his mind*.

35 **basement** (page 38)
a room at the bottom of a building, below the first floor. *Basements* do not usually have windows.

36 **got nothing to hide**—*to have nothing to hide* (page 39)
Lyle says that he's done nothing wrong. He's not hiding the truth.

37 **business cards** (page 41)
small cards which have your name, business address and phone number on them.

38 *casino* (page 42)
   a *casino* is a place where people go to *gamble*—to play games for money. There are *gambling tables* in casinos where people play different games. If someone does not obey the rules of the game, they are *cheating*. Las Vegas, in the state of Nevada, has many casinos. The law in this state allows gambling. In some other states in the U.S.A., gambling is against the law.

39 *the flu* (page 43)
   influenza. An illness where you have a fever and aches in your body, head and throat.

40 *drapes* (page 44)
   pieces of cloth that are pulled across a window.

41 *playing cards*—*to play cards* (page 44)
   playing a game with cards to win money. Sharon's job is to work at a gambling table (see above). When she has *dealt the cards*—given cards to each person who is playing the game—the card game begins.

42 *explosion* (page 47)
   when something breaks apart suddenly with a loud noise, this is called an *explosion*.

43 *hung up* (page 47)
   the person in Sharon's apartment has stopped speaking and put the phone down.

44 *rubber gloves* (page 47)
   gloves that are made of rubber. They are used in hospitals and factories to keep people's hands dry and clean. The rubber gloves that are used in hospitals are made from very thin rubber.

45 *briefcase* (page 47)
   a case used for carrying documents and papers.

46 *bathrobe* (page 48)
   a long, loose coat with a belt. Bathrobes are worn over nightclothes.

47 *bills* (page 49)
   the pieces of paper that you receive from a shop or a business. The *bill* has the amount that you have to pay, written on it.

48 *trailer* (page 51)
   a home on wheels. *Trailers* are less expensive than houses. A trailer can be pulled by a car or a truck to another place.

49 *shore* (page 51)
   the place where the water of a sea or a lake meets the land.

50 *tired of* (page 51)
   Kinsey often gets bored and angry when she asks people questions and they won't give her answers or information. She is *tired of trying to get information from them*. When several things have not happened

109

as she wants them to happen, Kinsey is *tired of being surprised.*

51 **making sense** (page 53)
if something *makes sense* to you, you can understand it. When you *make sense of something,* you succeed in understanding it. Kinsey had found out about things that had happened eight years ago. But she could not understand why this information was important.

52 **album** (page 55)
a special book which has photos stuck onto the pages. Families often keep *photo albums* with pictures of their relatives in them.

53 **job application** (page 59)
a letter or a form containing your personal details and qualifications which you use when you are asking someone for a job.

54 **victim** (page 65)
someone who is hurt or killed in a crime.

55 **made love**—*to make love with someone* (page 70)
have sex with someone.

56 **locksmith** (page 71)
a person who works with locks and keys. *Locksmiths* also make locks and keys.

57 **graduation** (page 73)
American students have secondary education in junior high schools from the ages of 12 to 14. They go to high schools from the ages of 14 to 18. They have a *graduation* when they pass their exams at the end of their studies at each of the two levels.

58 **parking lot** (page 78)
a flat open place where cars can be parked.

59 **carport** (page 78)
a place beside a house where a car can be parked. A *carport* has a roof but no walls.

60 **illegal** (page 81)
something which is against the law.

61 **alibis**—*alibi* (sing.) (page 82)
if a crime takes place somewhere and you are somewhere else at that time, you *have an alibi* for that crime.

62 **tranquilizer** (page 91)
a drug that makes you feel quiet and calm.

63 **fender** (page 97)
a wide band of rubber or metal that is attached to the front and the back of a car.

64 **trash bin** (page 100)
a large container for holding things that you no longer want—*trash* (rubbish).

Published by Macmillan Heinemann ELT
Between Towns Road, Oxford OX4 3PP
Macmillan Heinemann ELT is an imprint of
Macmillan Publishers Limited
Companies and representatives throughout the world
Heinemann is a registered trademark of Pearson Education, used under licence.

ISBN 978-1-405072-87-8

Illustrated by Annie Farrell
Original cover template design by Jackie Hill
Cover photography by Taxi

Printed in Thailand

2013 2012 2011
14 13 12 11 10